Also by Kate Banks

A novel by KATE BANKS and RUPERT SHELDRAKE

BOY'S BEST FRIEND

A novel by KATE BANKS and RUPERT SHELDRAKE

BOY'S BEST FRIEND

SQUARE FISH

FRANCES FOSTER BOOKS
Farrar Straus Giroux
New York

SQUARE
FISH

An imprint of Macmillan Publishing Group, LLC
175 Fifth Avenue
New York, NY 10010
mackids.com

Our books may be purchased in bulk for promotional, educational, or business use.
Please contact your local bookseller or the Macmillan Corporate and Premium Sales
Department at (800) 221-7945 ext. 5442 or by e-mail at
MacmillanSpecialMarkets@macmillan.com.

Library of Congress Cataloging-in-Publication Data
Banks, Kate, 1960– author.
    Boy's best friend / Kate Banks and Rupert Sheldrake.
        pages cm
    "Frances Foster Books."
    Summary: Lester has just moved to Cape Cod and is starting in a new school,
and George is missing his best friend who has moved away, but the two develop a
friendship and learn about scientific experimentation when they start working on
a school science project, testing psychic ability in dogs, based on an experiment
developed by Dr. Rupert Sheldrake.
    ISBN 978-1-250-07972-5 (paperback)
    ISBN 978-0-374-38009-0 (e-book)
    1. Dogs—Behavior—Juvenile fiction. 2. Extrasensory perception in animals—
Juvenile fiction. 3. Science projects—Juvenile fiction. 4. Schools—Juvenile
fiction. 5. Moving, Household—Juvenile fiction. 6. Friendship—Juvenile
fiction. 7. Cape Cod (Mass.)—Juvenile fiction. [1. Dogs—Fiction. 2. Animals—
Habits and behavior—Fiction. 3. Extrasensory perception in animals—
Fiction. 4. Science projects—Fiction. 5. Schools—Fiction. 6. Moving,
Household—Fiction. 7. Friendship—Fiction. 8. Cape Cod (Mass.)—Fiction.]
    I. Sheldrake, Rupert, author. II. Title.

PZ7.B22594Bo 2015
813.54—dc23
[Fic]
                                                                2014040380

Originally published in the United States by Farrar Straus Giroux
First Square Fish Edition: 2016
Book designed by Roberta Pressel
Square Fish logo designed by Filomena Tuosto

10 9 8 7 6 5 4 3 2 1

AR: 4.7

For all the animals that have inspired us

—K.B. and R.S.

A novel by KATE BANKS and RUPERT SHELDRAKE

BOY'S BEST FRIEND

1

"Moving is fun. Change can be positive." Lester Shoe repeated his mantra a dozen times, then a dozen more as he tried to fall asleep. A mantra was a group of syllables or words that carried power to make things turn out a certain way. It had been his mother's idea for him to try this. She chanted "Om" each morning for happiness and peace, and it seemed to work. She was always cheerful.

"Repeating a mantra quiets the mind," Lester's mother had said. "And it provides comfort in trying times." Then she had reached her palms skyward and bent forward into an upside-down V. Lester's mother was a yoga teacher and spent a lot of time in strange and unusual positions.

These were certainly trying times for Lester, who had moved from Denver to Cape Cod just after Easter and was going to start a new school in two days' time.

"A mantra can even unlock great virtues within," Lester's mother had added.

Lester liked the idea that there might be great virtues lurking within him waiting to be unleashed, and he wondered what those might be.

"Like what?" he'd asked.

His mother had said, "Oh, I don't know." But then she'd reeled off a list of attributes, some of which Lester felt he lacked. "Courage, confidence, patience, sacrifice, serenity."

"Oh," Lester had said, picking up a pencil and scribbling the words in his notebook, right next to a doodle of President Obama. Lester loved to doodle. In fact, doodling seemed to provide Lester with one of those virtues—serenity.

"But you need to be persistent for it to work," his mother had added.

Persistence. That was another quality that Lester felt he could use more of.

"Moving is fun. Change can be positive," Lester said to his dog, Bill Gates, who was curled up on the foot of Lester's new bed. "Moving is fun. Change can be positive." Eventually Lester's eyes closed and he fell asleep.

In the morning Lester sat up and looked around. "Where am I?" he said. The periwinkle-colored walls and the sparkling white window sashes were painfully unfamiliar. Lester tossed Bill Gates an old corduroy slipper. "I was dreaming about a spaceship," he said. "What were you dreaming? Do dogs even dream?"

Bill Gates bent his head to one side and looked at Lester in earnest. Lester imagined him saying, "Well, sure we do."

Lester petted Bill Gates on the crown of his head. "Of course you do," he said. "I mean, why wouldn't you?"

Bill Gates was a big dog—part mongrel, part golden retriever. Lester was four years old when he'd gotten him, and he was like a sibling, of which Lester had none.

Lester leaned over and nuzzled the dog's neck. "You're better than a brother or sister," he said. "Brothers and sisters fight. We never fight." Then he rolled off the bed and went to his desk. Lester glanced at the list of virtues in his notebook, then took the fat dictionary from his bookshelf. He turned to the word "virtue" and scanned the qualities in the definition. There were lots of them. Lester chose those that he felt were most important and added them to his list. Lester liked making lists. They made him feel organized and orderly—two other virtues. He had a list of his favorite movies, favorite songs, favorite places.

"Acceptance, Cleanliness, Honor, Joyfulness, Reliability, and Loyalty," Lester said aloud. Then he checked off the last one. "I might not be confident or patient," he said to Bill Gates. "But I think I'm pretty loyal, don't you?"

Lester closed his notebook and sketched a portrait of

himself on the cover—a thin figure flanked by a large dog. Lester was hardly thin. In fact, he was slightly overweight.

"Plump," he called himself. "But I'm sure I'll grow out of it," he continued to tell his mother.

Lester walked across the hall to the bathroom. He stood before the toilet and took aim. Back in Denver he could stand gazing out the window at the giant oak in the front yard and pee without looking. This toilet was a different shape and he had to pay attention lest he miss the mark. The window was in back of him so he stood facing a tile wall speckled with octopuses and starfish, which seemed to be staring at him.

Lester washed his hands and leaned over the faucet for a drink. He sloshed the water around in his mouth. "Even the water here tastes different from the water in Denver," he said, sighing.

Lester nudged Bill Gates down the stairs. Bill Gates had been lethargic of late and Lester had attributed it to the move.

"I know it's hard at the beginning," said Lester, repeating what his parents had told him. "You don't know other dogs. Everything is new and feels weird and different. But don't worry. You'll make new friends and you'll end up loving it here just as much as you love Denver." Lester paused. His mother was calling him.

"Lester, you forgot to take out the garbage last night. Would you please do it now?"

"Sure," said Lester. He went to the kitchen and stopped to pet the parrot housed in a cage next to the refrigerator.

"What's up, Carlos?" said Lester.

"What's up?" echoed Carlos. Lester guessed that was his mantra. Carlos knew at least fifty words, but those were his favorites.

Lester opened the refrigerator, took out a round of cheese, and popped it into his mouth.

"What's up?" chirped Carlos a second time.

"Why do I have to take out the garbage?" asked Lester.

"Because you don't have any brothers or sisters," said his mother, who was unloading the dishwasher.

"That's not my fault," murmured Lester, lifting the garbage bag and heading out the door followed by Bill Gates. Something about dropping the bag into the garbage can left him with an inexplicable feeling of emptiness.

Lester returned to the kitchen and sat down at the table. "I feel like I left something behind in Denver," he said.

"Like what?" asked his mother, smiling.

"Like part of me," said Lester. "The stuffing or something."

Lester's mother's smile rippled into a look of puzzlement. "How's that?" she asked.

Lester shrugged. "I just feel kind of empty."

Lester's mother's smile returned to normal. She seemed

happy about his emptiness. "Well, I'm sure you'll find plenty here to fill up those spaces," she said. "And you can start with this," she added, setting an omelet and two slices of buttered toast in front of him.

"I guess," said Lester, but he wasn't convinced. "Moving is fun. Change can be positive." He took a bite of the omelet, then looked at his mother. "Are you sure this mantra stuff works?" he asked.

Lester's mother nodded her head knowingly. "Yes," she said with confidence. That was one of her virtues.

Lester nodded back. Then the front door flew open and in came Lester's dad, back from an early morning jog. He was a sports journalist and he was the reason for the move. He'd gotten a new job.

"What a place for running," he said. "Boy does that feel great." Then he turned to Lester and gave him a high five. "What's new, big guy?" he asked.

What isn't new? thought Lester.

"Everything," he said. Then he started up the stairs chanting his mantra. "Moving is fun. Change can be positive." He looked back at his father, who was stretching, folding his calf to his buttock.

When he got to his room, Lester reached down and tried to touch his toes. He did twenty jumping jacks, then pushed the bed away from the wall and jogged five laps around it. But he didn't feel any better.

2

Later that same day, George Masson stood in line at the grocery store waiting to pay for a pack of atomic bubble gum, an amazing invention—at least George thought so—that fizzled in your mouth when you bit into it. The line was long. George was bored, so he began to stare at the back of the head of the man in front of him. He waited for the guy to turn around. After several seconds the man looked at George and George turned away.

When it was his turn to pay, George put the money on the conveyer belt and popped a piece of gum into his mouth, slipping the box into a pocket. Then he hopped on his bike and headed home. He stopped at a traffic light and stared at the back of a pedestrian's head. The pedestrian turned and looked at George strangely.

"Hi," said George.

"Hi," said the pedestrian.

George took a left onto Acorn Street and swerved

into his driveway. His older brother, Zac, was patching a tire on his bike. George stopped short and began staring at the back of his head.

Zac turned around. "What are you staring at, man?" he said.

"How'd you know I was staring?" asked George.

"Don't know," said Zac, going back to what he was doing. "I just did, and it's annoying." Then he added, "If you want to stare at someone, you can stare at Bart."

George turned to Bart, who sat at the top of the drive-way wagging his tail. He was the family dog, part border collie, part mongrel.

"Hey, big guy," George said, leaning down and scratching Bart under the chin.

"You shouldn't go around staring like that," said Zac. "It's rude. Besides people will think you're a weirdo."

"Rupert Sheldrake does it," said George. "He even does experiments about it."

"Who's Rupert Sheldrake?" asked Zac.

"He's my mentor," said George.

"You don't even know what a mentor is," said Zac.

"Yes I do," said George. "It's someone you want to be like."

George had heard about Rupert Sheldrake from Kyra, his best friend, who had moved after Christmas more than seven hundred miles away to North Carolina. George's attention was drawn to the green ribbon around his wrist that Kyra had given him before she left. She had one too, and they'd promised to never take them off, but to wait until they just wore away. George fingered the edge of the ribbon, hoping that little by little, as the fabric wore away, so would the feelings of sadness he felt at Kyra's leaving.

"Rupert Sheldrake wrote a whole book about staring," said George, pinching the ends of the ribbon between his forefinger and thumb. "He discovered that almost everyone can feel or sense or just know when someone is looking at them."

"He sounds like a weirdo," said Zac.

George didn't think Rupert Sheldrake was weird. But he had to admit that he was different from most scientists. Sheldrake thought that people and animals were connected by a knowing that had yet to be explained. He thought that maybe animals had abilities that had been lost or forgotten by humans. And he wasn't afraid to test his ideas. He wrote about homing pigeons, animals who anticipated natural disasters like earthquakes or tidal waves, cats who knew when they were about to be taken to the vet. And he'd written an entire book about dogs who knew when their owners were coming home.

"Sheldrake's experiments are important," said George.

Zac shook his head. "I fail to see what's so important about staring that you'd waste your time doing it."

"Because maybe it proves that people have a sixth sense or some other type of connection," said George.

"Oh, you mean like reading minds," teased Zac.

"It's called 'telepathy,'" said George.

"Telepathy isn't science," said Zac matter-of-factly.

"Yes it is," said George. "It's part of how animals and people behave. And that's science."

George blew a giant bubble, which snapped loudly as it broke.

"Cut that out," cried Zac.

"Anyway, Rupert Sheldrake asked me to participate in one of his experiments," said George.

"Oh, did he?" said Zac. He looked doubtful.

"Sort of," said George, lowering his eyes. "He has a Web site where he invites people to do his experiments. And I'm doing one for school starting tomorrow."

"You're just a kid," said Zac.

"He says kids can participate. He even wants them to," said George. "That's because he thinks that everyone can contribute something to science whether they are real scientists or not."

Zac rolled his eyes. "Well, I hope you're not doing the staring experiment," he said. "You'll drive people crazy."

George shook his head. "I'm doing the one about dogs who know when their owners are coming home. And Bart's going to help me." George rubbed the top of Bart's head. "Aren't you?" he said.

"That Sheldrake guy doesn't sound like he's doing science," said Zac. "He sounds like he's having fun."

"He is," said George. "That's the whole point. Science can be fun."

"You'll have to prove that one," said Zac, hopping onto his bike and cruising down the driveway.

3

George's younger sister, Vivien, skipped into George's room and sat down on the bed that George shared with a three-foot rubber snake, a beanbag monkey, and a stuffed tiger. George loved animals, real or pretend. At times, he'd even wondered if he wasn't meant to be one of them instead of a human.

"What's wrong?" said Vivien.

"Nothing's wrong," said George, who was sitting at his desk.

"Then why are you staring at the wall?" asked Vivien. "Are you depressed?"

George repeated that word to himself. De-pressed. It really seemed to describe how he felt since Kyra left, like a little bit of him had been pushed out and gone with her. "No," he said to Vivien. "I'm just thinking." George opened to page one of the logbook for the experiment he was going to do with Bart. The first entry looked like this:

DATE:

TIME GEORGE LEFT HOME:

MODE OF TRAVEL:

DESTINATION AND DISTANCE:

TIME GEORGE LEFT SCHOOL:

STOPS ALONG THE WAY:

TIME GEORGE STARTED FOR HOME:

TIME BART SEEMED TO START WAITING OR ANTICIPATING
GEORGE'S ARRIVAL:

TIME GEORGE ARRIVED HOME:

ANY OTHER COMMENTS OR OBSERVATIONS:

Vivien pushed her hands into the mattress and bounced up and down. She was eight years old, a girly girl who liked ballerina costumes and barrettes and shoes with sparkles. There were other girly girls at school, but George didn't quite know what to make of them. He preferred tomboys, like Kyra. She liked sports and science like George did, and loved doing experiments—and eating Kit Kats. The memory of Kyra's Kit Kats made George smile. He thought it was neat that simply thinking of something could make you smile. George thought about Kyra and all the fun they'd had to-

15

gether. It was Kyra's father who had gotten Kyra and George interested in experiments. He studied homing pigeons for a hobby.

Vivien jumped off the bed and peeked over George's shoulder at the open notebook on his desk. "What's that?" she asked.

"It's my logbook for an experiment I'm doing," said George.

Vivien ran her finger across the edge of the page where George had scribbled Rupert Sheldrake's name. "Who's Rupert Sheldrake?" she asked.

"A scientist," said George. "A biologist."

"What's a biologist?" asked Vivien.

"Someone who studies animals and their behavior," said George. "Stuff like that."

"Oh," said Vivien, still looking puzzled. She glanced down at George's ankles, which were wrapped one around the other beneath the chair.

"Your socks don't match," she said.

George looked down at his feet. One sock was dark blue, the other several shades lighter. He'd put them on without even noticing. "I wonder how that happened?" he said.

Vivien shrugged. "I guess you weren't paying attention," she said.

"Guess not," said George. He rarely paid attention to what he wore. He reached into his drawer in the morning and pulled out whatever he came to first. It didn't matter to him if he paired red with orange, or mixed plaids with stripes. It seemed to matter to other people, though, like his mother and Charlotte Peacock. Charlotte sat next to George at school, and she claimed to get a headache when he wore colors that clashed. George guessed it was because she didn't have any imagination. Or maybe he had too much.

George looked at his logbook. Suddenly he found himself imagining writing to Rupert Sheldrake. He wasn't sure what he would say. But he imagined Rupert Sheldrake responding. George smiled, then turned to Vivien. "If a total stranger wrote to you, would you write back?" he asked.

"Sure," said Vivien.

George realized that was a silly question. Vivien would write to anyone. She loved to write. She'd write to herself.

George's father's voice drifted up the staircase. "Dinner's ready," he called.

"Coming," George said. He followed Vivien down the staircase. Mr. Masson was in the kitchen putting the final touches on a platter of roast beef. He was an engineer by trade but he also loved to cook.

"Where's Mom?" asked George, taking the platter to the table.

"In here," cried Mrs. Masson, who was in her office off the kitchen. She was a pastry chef and catered from home.

Zac came into the kitchen and turned up the sound on his portable speakers.

Mrs. Masson sailed out of her office shaking her head. Her springy blond hair bounced off her shoulders, reminding George of a slinky. "Zac," she cried, stepping on Boots's tail. Boots was the family cat.

"Meowwww," wailed Boots.

"Mom," cried Vivien.

"Sorry, Boots," said Mrs. Masson. "Why is that cat always under my feet?"

Vivien slid under the table and gave Boots a pat. "Because she likes you, Mom."

George's father sat down at the head of the table. He opened his napkin and tucked it under his chin.

"You look like a baby," said Vivien.

"I spill like one too," said Mr. Masson, heaping George's plate with mashed potatoes and a mound of green peas.

"Don't forget my experiment starts tomorrow," George said to his mother. She had agreed to record when Bart went out to the front steps to wait for him. She'd been the first to notice that nearly every day, minutes before George's arrival, Bart stopped whatever he was doing and asked to be let out. Bart didn't do this with Vivien or Zac or Mr. or Mrs. Masson.

"Whoa," said Zac, making a T with his outstretched palms. "Time out. How do you know for sure that Bart knows when you're coming? It's probably a coincidence."

Zac shoveled a spoonful of mashed potatoes into his mouth.

"You're just a skeptic," said George.

"What's a skeptic?" asked Vivien.

"It's someone who doubts everything until there's absolute proof," said George. "Like Zac." George turned to his brother. "Maybe Bart has some way of sensing that I'm coming."

"And how are you going to prove that?" asked Zac.

"By doing that experiment I told you about," said George. "And by hundreds of other people doing the same thing."

Zac speared a pea with his fork. "But how can you prove it's something about Bart?" he said. "Maybe it's something about you, George." Zac leaned toward George and widened his eyes. "Oohh," he crooned.

Vivien looked at George with her big blue eyes. They reminded him of blueberries, the exact color and shape. "Maybe George is magic," she said. "Like Harry Potter."

George wasn't sure he liked being compared to Harry Potter. He didn't think he was any more magical than anyone else. But he did feel different at times. Or at least he thought he did. But how could he really know how anyone else felt?

George looked across the table at his older brother. Zac was blond like his mother, and thicker set. George was thin and dark. Zac liked synthesized music, computers, and electronics. George liked science, nature, and animals. How could two boys come from the same parents and be so different? What if he and Zac hadn't come from the same place? What if Bart was responding to something alien about George?

"You know, George," said Zac. "Sometimes I think you landed here from another planet."

"Could be," said George hesitantly.

Sensing his discomfort, George's mother came to the rescue. "I don't remember George arriving from outer space," she said. "I remember him coming full force at midnight on my thirty-second birthday after I'd eaten too much cake. Look, I don't know if Bart can read George's mind. But can anyone read mine?"

George could. "You want me to eat some peas," he said. He took a spoonful, looking down at the peas with their dented skins. They reminded him of tiny green golf balls. One pea dropped and bounced onto the floor, rolling silently to a stop. "If you write to a total stranger, do you think he'll write back?" he asked.

"Depends," said Zac. "Who are you thinking of writing to?"

"If you tell them you're depressed I bet they'll write back," said Vivien.

"George," said his mother. She looked concerned. "Are you depressed?"

"He misses Kyra," said Vivien.

"Would you be quiet, Viv," said George, fiddling with the tail of the green ribbon around his wrist.

"It's normal to be sad when a friend leaves," said George's mother. "But it will pass, George. I promise."

"You'll make new friends," said George's father. "Friends come and go. That's part of life."

"Just like vacations," said Vivien philosophically.

Zac cleared his throat. "In answer to your question, George," he said. "Don't expect a total stranger to write back."

George frowned.

Zac reached over and ruffled his hair. "Hey," he said. "I just don't want you to be disappointed."

"You think you know everything, Zac," said George. "I'm going to prove that really important people write to really unimportant people like me."

"I think you're important," said Vivien.

"Thanks, Viv," said George.

"I like your spirit," said Zac. "What do you want to bet?"

"Ten dollars," said George.

"You're on," said Zac, reaching out a hand to shake. He put down his napkin and stood up. "How about a game of Ping-Pong?"

"No thanks," said George. He helped clear the table, then took the stairs two at a time up to his room. He sat down at his desk and dropped his chin into his hands. Maybe he *was* depressed.

"Why is it so hard for some people to believe things?" he said out loud. Then he went to look for his mother.

"Can I use your computer?" he asked.

"Okay," she said. "But only fifteen minutes."

George sat down at the table his mother used for a desk. He opened up to Rupert Sheldrake's Web site. In the middle of the page was an e-mail address. George began to write.

Dear Dr. Sheldrake,

For my science class, I am doing your experiment about dogs who know when their owners are coming home. And I'm wondering if you would answer a few questions.

George paused. "Mom," he called. "Is twenty a few?"

"Twenty is more than a few," said his mother.

"What about a dozen?" said George.

"A dozen is twelve," said his mother.

"Oh," said George. "How much is a baker's dozen?"

"Thirteen."

"That's an unlucky number," George said to himself. Fourteen was better. George continued.

Like about fourteen. I was going to say thirteen but that's an unlucky number. I'm not superstitious but maybe you are. This is my first question: My brother, Zac, says it's just a coincidence that my dog, Bart, knows when I'm coming home from school. He says that even if I prove that Bart is waiting for me, I won't know why that is. I think maybe Bart is telepathic. Maybe I am. But even though it seems like that, how can we ever be sure? Sometimes, I wonder if we can we ever know anything for sure, even in science.

Sincerely,

George Masson

P.S. I love science and I think your experiments are really fun. Please write back.

4

On Monday morning Lester was up early, roused by the light of day trickling through the slats in the shades. He rolled over and hung his head over the side of the bed, feeling the blood rush to the roots of his hair. "Do you think this makes me smarter?" he said to Bill Gates. "More oxygen to my brain."

Lester slid off the bed and stood up. "Guess what?" he said. "I dreamed we walked all the way back to Denver."

Bill Gates had woken up too and was bathing, licking his fur with his long tongue (he was more fastidious about cleanliness than Lester). But he paused when Lester spoke.

"I love you, Bill Gates," said Lester.

Bill Gates went back to his bath while Lester thought how much easier washing would be if he had only to lick himself. He licked his forearm. It tasted salty.

"Time for breakfast," said Lester. He stuffed his notebook into his backpack and headed for the stairs with Bill Gates trailing behind.

"What's up?" chirped Carlos when Lester entered the kitchen.

"Good morning, Carlos," said Lester, although he wasn't sure what was good about it. In less than an hour he would be at a new school in a new classroom with a new teacher, surrounded by a bunch of new kids.

Lester's father was seated at the table reading the newspaper. He looked slick in a freshly pressed shirt, blazer, and tie. He always looked neat and tidy, even in his gym clothes. Lester guessed some people were just born that way. And he wasn't one of them. No matter how hard he tried, he always looked a little tousled—a stain on his shirt, a scab on his knee, a tuft of hair out of place. People in Denver didn't seem to mind. Lester wondered if anyone would mind here on Cape Cod.

Lester's father folded the newspaper and slapped it down on the table. "All ready for school?" he asked. He poured Lester a bowl of muesli and a glass of fresh-squeezed orange juice. He was convinced that the key to a successful day was a good breakfast.

Lester's mother glided into the kitchen in a green and pink chenille sweat suit.

"You look like a psychedelic caterpillar," said Lester.

"Why thank you," said his mother, smiling. "All ready for school?"

Lester smiled back halfheartedly. His palms had begun to feel sweaty. "I guess I am a little nervous," he admitted.

Lester's father turned and looked him straight in the eyes. Lester looked back at the small yellow and green flecks surrounding his father's pupils. They reminded him of fall in Denver.

"You know, Lester, dear," said his father. "In life you have to move forward. Don't look back."

"I know, I know," said Lester.

"I'm sure school will be fun," said his mother. "Your teacher seems lovely." Lester had met her when they'd visited Cape Cod after Christmas. And she did seem lovely—young and friendly. That reminded Lester of his list of virtues. He took his notebook from his backpack and added "Friendliness."

"Moving is fun," said Lester, repeating his mantra between mouthfuls of muesli. "Change can be positive."

"Don't worry. Be happy," said Lester's mother.

"Don't worry. Be happy," chirped Carlos. "Don't worry. Be happy." That was easy for him to say, thought Lester. He had nothing to do all day but sit on a stick and repeat what others said. Lester wondered if having nothing to do would make him happy. He doubted it.

Lester glanced at the clock. If he were in Denver he'd still be asleep because it was two hours behind there. Lester sighed. "The day will be over before I know it," he said.

"Oh, Lester," said his mother. "Don't wish your life away."

Lester knew she was right. If he thought like that, his whole life would be over before he knew it. And he wouldn't have enjoyed any of it.

"Would you like me to drop you at school?" asked Lester's mother.

"No thanks," said Lester. "I'm going to take my bike."

Lester's father nodded in approval.

Lester petted Bill Gates. "See you later, buddy," he said. Then he put his notebook back into his backpack and grabbed his lunch bag. His mother had made his favorite sandwich—ham on rye. "Bye," he said to his parents.

"Have a great day," said his mother.

"Ditto," said his father.

"Ditto," said Lester to himself. He sped down the sidewalk on his bike, chanting his mantra. "Moving is fun. Change can be positive." He looked down at his colored spokes. They created a kaleidoscope effect as they spun in endless circles, the same as they had in Denver. That made Lester feel good. When he got to school he pedaled over to the bike rack. There were two places left. Lester wondered in which to park. He couldn't make up his mind. "Eenie, meenie, miny, mo, out goes you," he said. Then he pulled into the spot on the end. And he went to find his seat in Ms. Clover's sixth-grade class.

5

George fed Bart his usual breakfast of cooked rice and nuggets with a bowl of fresh water. Then he stopped to count the holes in a pair of waffles his mother had made.

"Eat, George," said his mother. "You're going to be late to school."

George was finding it hard to think and eat at the same time. He wondered why this was. What did thinking have to do with eating, anyway? It seemed to George that if too many thoughts went into his head, there was no more room for food in his mouth. But George didn't think that was possible. Did other people have trouble eating and thinking?

"George," said his mother, waving a hand in front of his face. "Your breakfast is getting cold."

George stuffed the waffles into his mouth and washed them down with a glass of juice.

"Don't forget my experiment," George reminded his mother. Then he grabbed his backpack and hopped onto his bike. George liked riding to school—the sound of the wheels whipping the pavement, the world speeding past him. He turned into the schoolyard and headed for the bike rack. He usually parked in the last spot, but today there was another bike already there. George looked at the colored spokes. "Speak, spokes," he said. "What are you doing in my place?"

It wasn't officially his place, but he had been parking his bike there for two years. George pulled into the spot next to it, but it felt different. He was surprised how a little thing like that could make you feel different.

George took his seat in class. Ms. Clover had arranged the students' desks in an arc, like a crescent moon. George liked this configuration. He looked to his left. At the end of the arc was the seat where Kyra had sat at the beginning of last year. It usually was empty, but today there was someone in it.

"Class," said Ms. Clover. "We have a new student. I'd like you to welcome Lester Shoe, who's moved here all the way from Denver." She turned to Lester. "Maybe you could tell the class something about Denver," she said.

Lester thought for a moment. In Denver they sat in rows. And the desks had wells for pencils. The classroom smelled different too. Lester looked up. All eyes were directed his way.

"Denver has the longest street in America," said Lester at last.

"Really?" said Ms. Clover. "And how long is that?"

Lester wasn't sure. "I think about twenty-five miles," he said.

"Wow," said Ms. Clover.

Lester smiled. He had never had a teacher who said "wow"—not even in Denver.

At lunchtime, Lester was the first one to the cafeteria. He sat down at a table and took his ham sandwich from his bag. He had a packet of mustard, which he squeezed open, spattering the contents far and wide. A small blob landed on George, who was seated at the next table over.

"Sorry," said Lester. "It was an accident."

George looked down at his shirt, the one Kyra had given him, the one with "Save a Planet Ride a Bike" written across the front. "Does mustard stain?" he asked, noticing that Lester's breakfast was mapped out on his T-shirt—a splash of orange juice, an oat flake wedged in a wrinkle.

"I hope not," said Lester. He bit into his sandwich, then turned to George. "Want to know something weird?" he said.

George wasn't sure he did but he listened anyway.

"This sandwich is the same kind I ate in Denver,"

said Lester. "But it tastes different here on Cape Cod. Why do you think that is?"

George shrugged. He had no idea.

"I hope you're not mad about the mustard," said Lester.

George shook his head. "Mad" wasn't the right word. But he was annoyed and it wasn't because of the mustard. If Kyra had squirted him with mustard he would have laughed. But Kyra wasn't there. And that bothered him.

"I guess it tastes pretty good anyway," said Lester.

When Lester had finished his sandwich, he took a pack of mints from his shirt pocket. He always carried mints. He popped one into his mouth and then breathed in deeply. It felt cool and frosty in his throat. He personally thought that science had made a major breakthrough when it had discovered how to produce an entire winter day in a compact white candy.

"Want one?" he asked George, his attention caught by the green ribbon tied around George's wrist. Green was Lester's favorite color.

"No thanks," said George.

Lester looked around. "Anyone want one?" he asked.

"No thanks," said a big guy at the end of Lester's table. "I'm on a diet." He glared at Lester's slightly protruding belly. His look said it all.

The bell rang and Lester followed the crowd out to the playground. He sat down on a bench under a giant elm tree. It felt hard. It was wooden with slats. Why did they make benches with slats anyway, thought Lester. They weren't like that in Denver.

Lester looked around, hoping that maybe someone would notice him and come over and say hi. But no one did. They were all busy playing dodgeball, tag, or jump rope.

Lester mustered up the courage to stand up and shout, "The sky is falling." That was a game they played at his old school. It was a signal to run and hide. But no one was running or hiding now. He guessed they didn't know that game on Cape Cod. Lester sat back down on the bench and waited for the bell to ring. He was finding it hard not to wish the day away.

That afternoon they had science. "Lester," said Ms. Clover. "We've just started a new unit on animal behavior and some of the class are doing experiments with their pets. Do you have a pet?"

"I have a dog," said Lester. The thought of Bill Gates made him smile.

Ms. Clover smiled back. "George is doing an experiment on dogs who know when their owners are coming home," she said.

"My dog, Bill Gates, always knew when I was coming home back in Denver," said Lester. "But I don't know about here."

"So perhaps you could find out," said Ms. Clover. "George, why don't you explain your experiment to Lester during the break."

At break time, George got up and walked over to Lester's desk. He looked at Lester's notebook. It was covered with doodles. There was one in the corner of a guy who looked like Lester. Next to him was a dog.

"That's Bill Gates," Lester said. "What's your dog's name?"

"Bart," said George.

"Bart rhymes with fart," said Lester.

"And smart," said George, who preferred to think of Bart as intelligent rather than stinky.

"And heart," said Lester.

George tried to think of something that rhymed with Bill Gates. But he couldn't. Instead he took out his logbook. "The experiment was devised by a biologist named Rupert Sheldrake to see if some dogs have a knowing or connection to their owners. Kind of like telepathy. He has a Web site that you can check out."

"We studied telepathy in Denver," said Lester.

"Great," said George. "So you know what I mean. The idea is to record the time you set out for home from school—or it could be anywhere—for a period of days. When you get home you see if your dog is waiting in a particular spot. You have to ask someone at home to record how long the dog's been there so you can compare the time you left with the time your dog started waiting."

Lester nodded. That seemed easy enough. "How many days?" he asked.

"I'm doing it for twenty," said George. "But I'm skipping weekends because I'm not sure anyone will be home to help with the experiment." George tried to think if he'd forgotten anything. "Oh," he added. "And you have to vary the time each day so you know the dog isn't just reacting to habit."

"Okay," said Lester. He copied the details of the experiment in his notebook, while George looked at the list of words scribbled on the facing page.

"Those are virtues," said Lester.

"Oh," said George. He wondered why anyone would be making a list of virtues.

"I'm practicing them," said Lester, answering George's question as though he'd read his mind.

When school let out, George raced out the door and over to the bike rack. Lester was backing his bike out of George's old parking spot. He was talking to himself. He was actually repeating his mantra. "Moving is fun. Change can be positive."

"Oh, hi," he said when he saw George. "Sorry again about the mustard." He looked at George's shirt. The mustard reminded him of a splash of sunshine. "And thanks for explaining the experiment."

"No problem," said George.

Lester paused. "Well, I better get home and see if my dog is waiting for me," he said.

"Me too," said George. He checked his watch—3:03—then unlocked his bike and hopped on. As he sped home he found himself wondering why Lester's sandwich tasted different on Cape Cod than in Denver. Maybe things tasted different depending on where you were. Or maybe it depended on how you felt. That idea sent George's mind into a spiral. Did things taste the same to everyone? Did feelings feel the same? George parked his bike in the driveway and started up the walkway. Sure enough, Bart was waiting on the steps leading up to the porch.

George's mother checked her watch. "Bart's been waiting 9 minutes," she said.

"And it took me 11 minutes to get home," said George. "Thanks, Mom."

George leaned over to ruffle Bart's fur. "Hi, big guy. So you knew when I was coming." Then he went upstairs to his room to fill in his logbook.

"George," called his mother. "There's a message for you on the computer."

George raced back down the stairs. The message was from Rupert Sheldrake. He'd won the bet with Zac.

But that didn't seem so important. What mattered most was that Rupert Sheldrake had written back to him.

Dear George,

I would be happy to answer a few questions. If they are not too long then fourteen or fifteen would be fine. I am not superstitious where numbers are concerned, but many people here in England, where I live, are—so much so that there are office buildings and hotels that don't have a thirteenth floor.

In answer to your question, nothing is absolutely sure, even in science. Even the sun rising tomorrow isn't a certain fact, but it's very probable. Science works in terms of probabilities and of finding out what happens most of the time. Lots of people have dogs that seem to anticipate their owner's arrival, going to the door or window and waiting well before their owners get home. Is it just a coincidence, as skeptics say? The only way to find out is by making detailed observations. It's no use just arguing about it. That's why evidence is so important in science.

It may seem to you like your dog knows when you are coming home. But you would have to see if your dog favors a particular spot—it could be inside or out—or only goes there when you are about to arrive. And your dog would have to repeat this behavior with some consistency. If your dog does this repeatedly before your arrival, and even when you come home at different times of the day, that would suggest that it's really responding to your returning in some way or another.

I'm sure your brother might then argue that this is because your dog hears your footsteps or a car or a school bus. But you can check this by varying the way you get home. Perhaps you could take your bike or have someone drive you. If your dog still reacts, this would lend evidence to the idea that he's picking up on something about your intention to come home.

Good luck with your experiment and let me know how it goes.

Best wishes,
Rupert Sheldrake

George turned off the computer and went to find Zac. He was in the garage with Vivien, adjusting the handlebars on her bike.

"Zac is fixing my bike so I can ride it to school instead of taking the bus," said Vivien. Vivien hated the school bus.

"Mom isn't going to let you ride your bike to school," said George.

"In a couple years she will," said Vivien. "So I'm practicing."

George turned to Zac. "Rupert Sheldrake wrote back to me. I won the bet."

"Woooo," said Zac. "Fair and square." He reached into his wallet for a ten-dollar bill.

"What are you going to do with it?" Zac asked, handing George the money.

"I think I'll just save it," said George.

"See, George," said Vivien. "You're more important than you think." She looked happy.

George went back up to his room to text Kyra. "Guess what?" he wrote. "I e-mailed Rupert Sheldrake and he e-mailed me back."

Two minutes later, Kyra texted back three smilies, followed by "What did he say?"

"He's going to answer some of my questions about animal behavior," wrote George. Then he added, "There's a new guy sitting in your old seat. He's from Denver."

Kyra wrote back, "I'd like to go to Denver."

George sighed. Kyra was always eager to explore new places and things. Even though she'd been sad to leave Cape Cod, she'd been excited to move to North Carolina.

"I can't wait to see what it's like," she'd said. Then after she moved, she'd texted him about the way the people there talked and what they ate. "It's really different from the Cape," she'd written. But she seemed to like it there. George wondered if the ability to like was infinite—if you could like new things, but keep liking the old things just as much. He hoped so.

6

When Lester arrived home that afternoon, Bill Gates was sitting on the stone walkway behind the front gate.

"You were waiting for me, weren't you?" said Lester, giving the dog a cuddle. "Too bad that dog experiment didn't start today."

Lester's mother was looking at paint samples for her new yoga space off the kitchen. She'd named it the Sunshine Studio and decided to paint it a shade of blue. "How was your day?" she asked.

"Okay," said Lester. "But it's a lot different from Denver. Some of the kids are on diets."

"Diets?" said Lester's mother. She furrowed her brow, but her smile quickly returned.

"I have a science project that seems pretty fun," said Lester. "Dogs who know when their owners are coming home. I have to see if Bill Gates waits for me here after school like he did in Denver. And I have to keep a logbook for twenty days."

"That does sound like fun," said Lester's mother.

"But I need someone to record when Bill Gates goes out to wait for me," said Lester.

"I'd be happy to do that," said Lester's mother.

"You have to be precise though," said Lester.

"I can be very precise," said Lester's mother.

Lester knew his mother could be precise. That was another of her virtues.

"Good," said Lester. "I guess I'll start tomorrow then. George started today."

"Who's George?" asked Lester's mother.

"A guy I met at school," said Lester. He went up to his room and made a logbook for his experiment, like George had shown him. When he was finished he took his notebook, turned to his list of virtues, and added "Precision." Then he put a check beside Courage. It had taken a lot of courage to get through the first day at a new school.

7

On Tuesday, Ms. Clover asked the class to take out their history books. She began talking about names and how in ancient times they'd often denoted something about a person.

"Oftentimes people took their names from their professions," she explained. "Lester Shoe's ancestors may have been cobblers, for example."

George looked down at his own name penciled on a piece of masking tape on the corner of his desk. Masson. Maybe his ancestors had been bricklayers. Then George remembered that "mason" had only one "s." His name had two. So maybe my ancestors couldn't spell, he thought.

Lester raised his hand. He'd noticed something interesting and wanted to share it with the class. Sharing was something they did in Denver. Lester wondered if it was the same here. He took a deep breath. "Did you ever notice that you have the word 'love' in your name?" he said.

Someone snickered. Then Ms. Clover laughed out loud. "No I didn't," she said.

George looked down at his own name again. Masson. Oops, he had the word "ass" in his name. He'd never noticed that before, and he wished he hadn't now. He hoped no one else did. If only Lester hadn't mentioned the word "love" in Ms. Clover's name, then George would never have noticed the "ass" in his name.

Lester glanced around the room. He closed his eyes, trying to remember the faces, then opened them again. He did this a few times. He wanted to memorize the faces so when he saw his classmates in the hallway he could say hello.

"Are you okay?" asked the girl next to him. Her name was Sheila.

"I'm fine," said Lester. "Thanks for asking."

The rest of the day, Lester made an effort to say hello to anyone he recognized. Some of the kids said hi back. But most of them looked at him like he was a weirdo.

On the way out of school, Lester even said hi to someone he'd never seen before.

"Do I know you?" the guy answered.

"I don't think so," said Lester. "I was just saying hi."

The guy nodded. "Gotcha," he said.

When Lester got to the bike rack, George was already there.

Lester checked his watch. It was 3:01. "I'm starting

my experiment with Bill Gates today," he said. "I wonder if he'll be waiting."

"Good luck," said George, backing his bike out of the rack.

"Thanks," said Lester. He pedaled off, trying to focus on home. But for some reason images of Denver kept appearing in his mind. When he got home at 3:11, Bill Gates was in the backyard sunbathing.

"He's been there all afternoon," said Lester's mother.

Lester gave Bill Gates a gentle nudge. "Didn't you know I was coming?" he said. Lester thought maybe it was because he hadn't been precise enough when thinking of home. He'd thought about Denver when he meant to be thinking about Cape Cod.

Lester went up to his desk and filled in his logbook halfheartedly. Then he turned to his list of virtues and zeroed in on Precision. "Moving is fun. Change can be positive."

Meanwhile, George had pedaled home as fast as he could, setting a record. When he arrived, Bart was waiting on the porch steps.

"He's been there 8 minutes," said George's mother. George checked his watch. It was 3:10.

George went up to his room to fill in his logbook. He tried to focus on dogs, but for some reason his own name kept pushing into his thoughts. He wondered if you could change the spelling of your name.

8

When Lester went down to the kitchen on Wednesday morning, his mother eyed him from head to toe. "Don't you look nice today," she said.

"Thanks," said Lester, pouring himself some cereal, then carefully closing the box and returning it to the cupboard. He'd made the decision to be more precise right before going to bed. And he'd already started to be so, aiming carefully at the toilet in the new bathroom. When he'd gotten dressed he'd made sure that his clothes were in order and his hair was combed. After breakfast he walked to school, reminding himself to think about home more precisely when school got out.

Lester was more precise than usual when he did his math exercises. And when he put mustard on his sandwich at lunchtime he was careful not to squirt anyone. He was more precise about who he was friendly with too. He only said hello to those people he recognized. But still, not all of them spoke back.

Lester walked home from school repeating his mantra. "Moving is fun. Change can be positive," he said as he thought precisely of his new house with the faded gray clapboards.

Lester arrived at 3:24 and Bill Gates was waiting on the walkway behind the gate.

"Hey, so you knew I was coming," said Lester, letting himself into the yard.

"He's been waiting 19 minutes," said Lester's mother, who was cleaning the windows on the front door.

Lester looked at his watch. He'd started home 21 minutes ago. He ran upstairs and carefully filled in his logbook. Then he looked out the window above his desk. There was a tree and it had new buds sprouting on it. They made Lester feel hopeful. He picked up his pencil, opened his notebook, and drew the tree in great detail. Then he turned to his list of virtues and checked off Precision.

Four blocks away, George was filling in his logbook. He'd left school at 3:05, taken the long way home on his bike, and arrived home at 3:22. Bart had been waiting 12 minutes.

"Way to go, Bart," said George. "I hoped you'd be here and you are." But then he wondered what might have happened if he hadn't hoped.

Dear Dr. Sheldrake,

Thank you for responding to my first question. Here is my second question. I'm having a hard time not hoping that my dog, Bart, will be waiting for me after school. I wonder how I can turn off my expectations. Are real scientists able to turn off their expectations? If so, maybe you can tell me how. Also I wonder if my family's expectations affect my experiment. I guess they must. Do you think if people have different expectations, they cancel each other out?

Sincerely,

George Masson

Dear George,

All scientists have expectations when they do experiments. If they didn't have any, they wouldn't bother to do the experiment. Usually they are testing a hypothesis, which is a kind of guess about the way things are. They can't possibly work as scientists without expectations, and nor can you. Either Bart is going to be waiting for you or he isn't, and whether you hope he is waiting will only affect him if he can pick up your thoughts, which is what this experiment is about anyway. So I don't think your expectations are a problem.

There could be a problem if people at home know when you're coming. If they expect that you're going to arrive at 4 p.m., for example, they might start behaving differently and Bart might notice this and start waiting because of their expectations. So in this experiment it's important that your family doesn't know exactly when you're coming home. Of course it's possible that skeptical expectations (like your brother's) could affect Bart if someone is at home with him thinking negative thoughts. They might put Bart off or distract him. So again, the best way to deal with positive or negative expectations of people at home is to come home at a random hour. Of course this would have to be arranged in such a way that your parents don't get worried and send out a search party.

Let me know how you get on.

Best wishes,

Rupert Sheldrake

9

On Thursday George had a dentist appointment after school.

"Who's going to watch for Bart?" he said.

Zac volunteered. "I'll do it. I'm home by three. Then Mom can leave to pick you up at school."

George hesitated, remembering what Rupert Sheldrake had written him. George wasn't sure he wanted someone who didn't believe in telepathy to be part of the experiment, but then he decided it was actually a good idea. If Bart did go out to the step when Zac was there, then he would still be responding to George. "Okay," said George.

"I'll even do it for free," Zac said, laughing.

"Thanks," said George. He grabbed his lunch and backpack and headed for the door.

"Can I walk with you?" asked Vivien, raising her eyebrows in that way that made it hard for George to say no.

"Don't you want to take the bus?" asked George hopefully.

"No," said Vivien. "I take it all the time. Please. You hardly ever walk."

"George," said his mother.

George sighed. "All right," he said.

He headed down the driveway with Vivien in tow. She was wearing her lemon-yellow canvas sneakers with white trim—the kind you saw tossed on beaches in the summer in all colors of the rainbow. George looked at them, then shifted his gaze off into the distance.

"What are you doing, George?" asked Vivien.

"Nothing," said George. "Just thinking."

"About what?" said Vivien.

George was thinking about names again. Kyra's last name was Joyner. And he'd just realized that she had the word "joy" in her name. A sensation of warmth like the midday sun surged through George's body. "I was thinking about Kyra," he said.

"Is she your girlfriend?" asked Vivien.

That question annoyed George. Maybe it was because he didn't know how to answer it. What did it really mean? He thought of the things he'd liked about Kyra when he'd first met her. The spray of freckles across her cheeks. The way she could touch the tip of her tongue to her nose. The way she bounced when she walked. But what he liked most was the way she thought. Like he did. Was he in love with her? George remembered one of the first things Kyra had said to him.

"Do you think you can feel someone's presence when they aren't around?" She hadn't even waited for him to answer. "I do," she'd said.

At the time that had made perfect sense to George. But now as he stood struggling to connect to Kyra, her presence was the furthest thing from his grasp.

"She's not my girlfriend," said George at last. "She's just a friend."

George left Vivien with her classmates and crossed the playground. Lester was playing tetherball with Sean Hanlon, the biggest guy in the class. George stopped to watch. Sean banged the ball and sent it spiraling around the pole.

"You're good," Lester said.

"You're not," Sean answered. Lester guessed politeness was not one of Sean's virtues. But he kept up the game until he'd lost 21 to 2.

"Better luck next go," said Sean, banging the ball into the pole one last time.

"Sure," said Lester.

The bell rang and the students went into their classrooms.

Ms. Clover handed out a math sheet with word problems. For one of them Lester had to figure out the time difference between New York and Paris. That got him thinking of Denver. He looked at his watch. In Denver the sun was just coming up. In Denver he was two hours younger. That was a weird thought. But the strangest thing about it was that Lester couldn't get it out of his head, not until the afternoon when Sheila had a little accident.

It was art day and Ms. Clover had asked them to cut out silhouettes of one another. Sheila began to do Lester, but halfway through she pinched her finger on the scissors. It started to bleed. Lester began to feel queasy. He hated the sight of blood.

"Here," he said, reaching into his pocket and offering Sheila one of the napkins he kept for emergencies, like cake and pies. But the finger kept bleeding. Lester was relieved when Ms. Clover asked Charlotte to take Sheila down to the nurse, and he got to do a silhouette of George. Lester studied George's profile then traced an image of it on a piece of bright red construction paper.

"That's pretty good," said George.

"Thanks," said Lester, remembering that politeness was a virtue.

When the class had finished, Ms. Clover taped the silhouettes to the board and the students tried to guess who was who. Everyone recognized George, but no one recognized Sheila's half-finished portrait of Lester.

Lester lingered at the tetherball before starting home. He was hoping that Sean might come by and ask for another game. But he didn't. Lester gave the ball a punch, then walked over to the bike rack. He wondered if maybe George would be there. But he wasn't. Lester checked his watch. It was 3:16. He hopped on his bike and pedaled off just as George's mother pulled up to the curb.

George climbed into the car and looked out the window. A guy on a bicycle was speeding off down a side street, his hands stretched out to his sides like a bird. It took George a few minutes to realize that it was Lester.

George's dentist appointment lasted 30 minutes. "No cavities," said George to his mother. He spun a pinwheel that he'd gotten out of the treasure chest that the dentist kept treats in for exemplary patients. George had been an exemplary patient.

"Aren't you a little old for that?" his mother asked.

"I got it for Viv," said George. He checked his watch. It was 4:01. "This will be a really good test for Bart," he said.

When they pulled into the driveway, Bart was waiting on the porch steps and Zac and Vivien were playing Ping-Pong in the garage.

"Bart's been there for 8 minutes on the nose," said Zac. George looked at his watch. It was 4:12.

"That proves that Bart knew I wasn't coming home right after school," said George. He handed Vivien the pinwheel. "For you," he said.

"Freaky," said Zac, who looked a little puzzled.

"Zac always lets me win," said Vivien, putting down her paddle and blowing into the pinwheel. George picked up the paddle.

"I won't let you win," said George.

Meanwhile Lester had arrived home at 3:27. It had taken him 11 minutes on his bike.

"Bill Gates has been waiting 7 minutes," said Lester's mother, pushing open the front gate. Bill Gates trotted up to Lester.

"So you knew I was coming," said Lester, rubbing Bill Gates under the chin.

Lester's mother smiled widely. "It certainly seems that way," she said. "How was your day?"

"Okay," said Lester. "But Sheila didn't have such a good day."

"Who's Sheila and why not?" asked Lester's mother.

"A girl in my class," said Lester. "She cut her finger on some scissors."

"I hope not badly," said Lester's mother.

"It could have been worse," said Lester.

"It could have been worse," repeated Lester as he climbed the stairs and went to his room to fill in his logbook. "I could have cut myself." But that thought didn't make him feel much better. In fact, he felt like he had cut himself. But not his finger. It was deeper inside, somewhere where he couldn't reach.

Lester went down to the basement and began searching through a box he'd brought from Denver.

"Are you missing something?" called Lester's father, who was at his desk writing.

"Denver," mumbled Lester.

"What was that?" said his father.

"My boomerang," said Lester. He found it and took it out to the backyard. "What do you think, Bill Gates?" he said. "If I could throw this all the way to Denver, would it return to me?"

That evening George texted Kyra. "Did you know you have the word 'joy' in your name?" he wrote. He was about to punch the send button when he changed his mind and pressed delete. He'd realized that the moment Kyra read that, she would think of his name and what words were in that.

George then wrote, "Did you ever notice that Ms. Clover had the word 'love' in her name?" But he erased that too. Finally he wrote, "Did I tell you the new guy's name is Lester Shoe? He loves mustard and he talks to himself. He took my bike spot. And he has a dog named Bill Gates. What kind of a guy do you think would name his dog Bill Gates?"

10

On Friday Lester decided to change a variable for his experiment. He took his mother aside. "I'm coming home really late today," he said. "George said the results of the experiment are more accurate if you don't know exactly when I'm coming. Then you don't expect me. If you expected me you might behave differently and Bart might figure out that I'm coming."

"I see," said Lester's mother, looking up from the cookbook she was reading. She was smiling, but she'd wrinkled her forehead in a series of gentle waves so that Lester wasn't quite sure if she really did see.

"What are you making?" he asked.

"I thought I would make lasagna," she said. That was one of Lester's favorite meals.

"Great," said Lester, his mouth beginning to water.

When Lester got to school, George's bike was already in the rack. Lester looked at the sticker on the cross-bar. "There is no Planet B," it read. Lester liked that.

"Moving is fun. Change can be positive," he said as he crossed the playground.

Lester took his seat in class and opened his notebook. He skimmed his list of virtues. "Patience," he whispered. "Moving is fun. Change can be positive."

"Are you talking to me?" said Sheila.

"No," said Lester. His attention was drawn to her wounded finger, which was covered with a Band-Aid.

"Then who are you talking to?" Sheila asked.

"No one," said Lester. Sheila looked disappointed, but Lester didn't notice. He was too busy wishing away the day.

"TGIF," Lester said to himself. He was glad it was Friday, thankful that he'd made it through his first week of school. The problem was he was doing just what his mother had told him not to do—wishing his life away, hoping that the weekend would come sooner.

After school, Lester spotted George pulling out of the bike rack. He stopped to read the bumper sticker another time. "I like your sticker," he said.

"A friend gave it to me," said George.

"I like your friend then," said Lester, sitting down on the curb. "I'm hanging out for a while before going home. Testing Bill Gates. He was waiting for me yesterday."

George pulled his bike out of the rack. He checked his watch—3:03. "I bet he'll be waiting today too," he added before speeding off.

Bart was waiting when George got home.

"Six minutes," said George's mother.

Lester lingered on the playground a while, then took baby steps home, stopping in front of his neighbor's house. He looked at the tall hedges with their small pinecones. Then he peeked through them. An older lady was out back puttering around a toolshed. She opened the door to the shed and stepped in. Lester could hear noises coming from inside. It sounded like a shuffle. Suddenly the lady came out of the shed and quickly pulled the door closed.

Maybe she's hiding someone in there, thought Lester. Maybe she's a criminal. Lester thought of his neighbors back in Denver—the Bristows. They weren't criminals. They had twin girls, eight years old, who were really cute. Every spring the Bristows had a barbecue and invited all the neighbors.

Lester turned away from his neighbor's house, focusing on his new home on Cape Cod. "Here I come," he said. Two minutes later, Lester walked through the front gate.

"Bill Gates just came out four minutes ago," said Lester's mother.

"Can't fool you, can I?" said Lester to Bill Gates. Lester went up to his room and filled in his logbook. Then he took his notebook and began sketching. He drew

Sheila with a Band-Aid on her finger. Then he drew himself with a Band-Aid on his heart.

George waited until dessert—lemon meringue pie, one of his mother's specialties—before mentioning what had been on his mind the entire week.

"I was thinking—" he said.

Zac interrupted him. "That's your first mistake," he said between bites of foamy meringue.

George ignored his brother. "Ms. Clover has the word 'love' in her name," he said. "What do you think that means?"

"Why does everything have to mean something?" asked Zac.

"We have a word in our name too," said George. He didn't wait for them to guess, but blurted it out. "Ass."

"George," cried his mother.

"We have a lot of words in our name," Zac reminded George. He began to list them. "Son, as, mass, on."

"Too many, I think," said George. "Maybe we should take out one of the s's."

"Why would we do that?" asked Mr. Masson.

George shrugged. "It's just an idea," he said.

"I can't think of a better way to complicate our lives," said Mrs. Masson.

George's father folded his napkin and rose from the

table. "Well I'm proud to be a Masson," he said. "Ass or no ass."

"Me too," said Vivien.

"Me too," said Zac.

"Me too," said George weakly.

After dinner, George went up to his room and got out his dictionary. He looked up "sheldrake." A sheldrake was a gooselike duck slightly larger than a mallard, with mostly black-and-white plumage and a red bill. George wondered how Rupert Sheldrake had ended up with that name. His relatives couldn't have been ducks, but maybe they'd owned ducks. Or liked ducks.

George turned to the A's and scrolled down the page to "ass." Ass: a stupid, obstinate, or perverse person; any of several African or Asian mammals; buttocks.

"Ass," said George out loud. "Ass, ass, ass." He couldn't help but think how Kyra might react to what he was doing. She would probably laugh. That's because she had "joy" in her name and not "ass."

11

Saturday morning Lester decided to take Bill Gates to the marsh.

"Let's see what this place is like," he said to the dog. Lester had never seen a marsh, but everyone on Cape Cod seemed to think it was special.

Lester gazed at the long extensions of water that stretched their fingers inland. In the distance an island bubbled eerily from the surface of the waves. Lester started along one of the paths that threaded through the low-lying brush toward the sea. At first Bill Gates stayed by Lester's side, but as they neared water he broke loose, diving headfirst into the patches of sea lavender and cordgrass.

"Hey," cried Lester. "Wait for me." Lester took a deep breath. He could smell the sea wafting his way.

"Something stinks," he said. "It's not you, Bill Gates. Or me, I hope." Lester was reminded of how people couldn't really tell when they smelled bad. Everybody seemed to like their own odor. That was funny. Lester guessed it was kind of the same way that everybody liked their own city—like he liked Denver.

Lester's cheeks began to feel damp. A wave of fog had drifted in suddenly, billowing around him, blurring his vision. It was kind of spooky. Overhead, a bird screeched and Lester jumped backward, sinking into the mud.

Lester looked down at his feet. "This place should be called the mush, not the marsh," he said. That got Lester thinking about marshmallows. Lester loved marshmallows. But how could anyone love the marsh? What was so special about wet, spongy earth? Then Lester remembered that he hadn't always liked marshmallows. They'd just sort of grown on him.

Lester stepped back onto solid ground. He picked up a stick and tossed it. "Fetch," he cried. Bill Gates raced ahead, retrieved the stick, and brought it back to Lester.

"Good boy," cried Lester.

Lester stopped to watch the birds dip and dive across the sky. He spread his arms and pretended to be one of them. He could almost imagine how it must be to fly. For a moment he thought he might even take off.

Lester repeated his mantra. "Moving is fun," he said. "Change can be positive."

"I wonder if the marsh might grow on us," Lester said to Bill Gates as they walked home. "I doubt it."

When Lester neared his house he spotted his neighbor hurrying alongside the hedge with a parcel in her arms. Lester moved closer, squinting through the foliage. She ducked into the toolshed just like she had the day before. Lester could hear her voice wafting his way. "Ssh, sshh, that's a good boy."

Bill Gates barked once, then sat waiting for Lester.

Lester allowed his imagination to get the better of him. "Maybe she's a kidnapper." Lester wondered what the crime rate was on Cape Cod. In Denver they didn't have much crime at all.

Bill Gates sat patiently for several minutes but then became restless. He nudged Lester forward.

"How was the marsh?" asked Lester's mother when they got home.

"Mushy," said Lester. "It reminds me of marshmallows."

"You love marshmallows," Lester's mother said.

"Yup," said Lester, opening a cupboard. "Do we have any?" Lester reached into the back and pulled out a plastic bag. There was one marshmallow left. He popped it into his mouth. "I think our neighbor, the old lady, is hiding someone or something in her toolshed," he said. "Do you think she could be a criminal?"

Lester's mother laughed. "You mean Mrs. Robarts?" she said. "A criminal? Why, she seems like a sweet old woman."

"Things aren't always what they seem," said Lester. His friend Bernie back in Denver used to say that all the time. Lester thought it sounded good, but he hadn't really stopped to think about what it meant. "And," he added, "she has the word 'rob' in her name." That had just occurred to him.

"Hmm," hummed his mother, but she didn't seem to be listening.

Just as Lester was arriving home, Bart was following George around the back of the house, toward the marsh. When they'd first gotten Bart, Zac had promised to share the walks, but now he claimed to be too busy. George guessed that happened when you turned fifteen. Anyway, the walks fell to him, but he didn't mind. He always had a good chat with Bart.

George picked up a piece of driftwood and tossed it. He thought it was neat how things were taken out to sea, swept up in its maelstrom, and returned to shore in never-ending cycles—one day a starfish, the next a sea sponge or a horse mussel. It made him think of the boomerang Kyra had given him when she left.

"To remind you that I'll be back," she'd said. "If only just to visit."

Bart ran ahead, retrieved the driftwood, and dropped it at George's feet.

"Good boy," said George, giving Bart a pat.

Bart scampered through the sea lavender and marsh mallow. His ears stiffened as he registered a distant cry. The birds were returning to the marsh after the long winter, nesting in colonies dug in the tops of steep banks. A great blue heron had taken up residence in an abandoned beaver dam. Kyra had taught George the names of the marsh birds. She knew them all by heart.

George squinted into the distance toward a weathered outbuilding that leaned into the breeze. That was where Kyra's father had kept his pigeon loft. But he'd dismantled the loft when they'd left.

One of the pigeons had been Kyra's. Alabaster was her name. She'd flown off one morning and never returned. After Kyra left, there had been moments when George could picture Kyra and Alabaster as clearly as if they were really there. But as time passed, the feeling had dissipated.

"It's funny how feelings evaporate," George said, catching up to Bart. "Kind of like water." Bart tilted his head and looked at George with his chocolate-colored eyes in a way that made George feel that he understood everything he said. George suspected that he might. He was convinced that sometimes Bart listened to him more attentively than even his own parents did.

George sighed, leaning into a tree that seemed to shiver in the breeze. He lifted his arms and shivered too. Then he lowered his arms back down. He thought about his conversation with Vivien and how he had wondered if you could feel someone's presence after they'd left.

As they followed the path home, Lester popped into George's head. George was remembering something Lester had said. "Bart rhymes with heart," he said aloud.

Dear Dr. Sheldrake,

I'd like to ask you a question that's not about dogs or animals—unless you consider people animals. Do you? But it's a question that has something to do with telepathy. Do you think you can feel someone's presence when they are no longer there? How is this possible? Sometimes I feel the presence of people who have left, and it seems like they are almost there.

Sincerely,
George Masson

P.S. Did you know there's a bird called a sheldrake?

Dear George,

We share many common traits with animals, such as sensory perceptions, habits, reproduction (and I guess names too!). And we are part of the natural order and affect it. So yes, I think we are animals.

I suppose whenever we remember somebody, in some way they are there, but of course we know it's a memory.

But if you feel someone's presence when they've gone away is it more than memory? I don't really know.

Rather mysteriously, this sometimes happens when people have died. When people have been married for a long time, of course they know each other very well. Studies in Britain of people who have lost a husband or wife showed that about half of them felt the presence of the person who had died at least once after their death. Sometimes they even saw them or heard their voice. But was this due to memory? Or might it have been the dead person trying to come back to say that they were all right? No one really knows. But the fact that you feel the presence of someone who's gone away certainly shows that you have a connection of some kind. Whether or not that person can feel your thoughts about them is another question.

I do know that "sheldrake" is a bird name, like many other names in the English language.

Best regards,

Rupert Sheldrake

12

On Monday Ms. Clover reviewed the work they'd done on prehistoric man.

"Neanderthal man was physically more robust than modern man and had a larger head," she said.

George looked to his left, at Charlotte Peacock's head. Her long, silky black hair swung from side to side in one big sheet when she moved. It reminded George of a paintbrush. George continued to stare but Charlotte didn't turn around. Charlotte never turned around no matter how long George kept his eyes on her. George wondered why that was. Nearly everyone else seemed to turn around.

Suddenly George asked himself why he couldn't have a bird for a last name. He tried to imagine how he would feel as George Eagle or George Hawk. The idea made him laugh.

Charlotte turned to George. "What are you laughing at?" she said.

"Nothing," said George. He hoped she couldn't read his thoughts.

"Does anyone have any questions?" asked Ms. Clover.

George had lots of questions. *How can all my thoughts fit into my head? Do thoughts take up space? Did Neanderthal men have more thoughts because they had bigger heads?*

Suddenly George looked across the arc of seats to where Lester was sitting and fixed his eyes on the side of Lester's head, on his curly blond hair. When Lester turned around, George shifted his attention to the illustrations of Neanderthal man on a work sheet in front of him. He wondered if Neanderthal men knew when they were being looked at. He thought they must have when they were hunting. They must have known when they were being watched by wild animals.

George began folding a piece of scrap paper. He had no idea what he would make, but slowly the paper took the form of a small jet. George wanted to see if Ms. Clover would turn around. Sure enough she did.

"George," she said. "Put the plane away, please. They didn't have airplanes 350,000 years ago." George put away the plane. He wondered if teachers had a special kind of telepathy. They always seemed to know when there was trouble. It was like they had eyes in the back of their heads. Maybe people in certain professions developed telepathic capacities because it helped them in their work and allowed them to do a better job. George wondered if Rupert Sheldrake would agree.

After school George bumped into Lester playing hop-scotch next to the bike rack.

"My teacher in Denver had eyes in back of her head too," said Lester.

George paused. Had Lester read his mind? "I think all teachers do," he said.

"And mothers," added Lester.

George looked down at Lester's feet. They looked funny. His shoelaces were too long so he'd wrapped them around his ankles and tied them in the front so he wouldn't trip.

"Where's your bike?" asked George. The last slot in the rack was empty. There were no colored spokes.

"I'm giving Bill Gates the ol' slip again today," said Lester. "I'm walking home a different way so I'll get there at a different time."

"How's the experiment going, anyway?" asked George.

"So far so good I guess," said Lester. "Bill Gates has been waiting for me three days out of four. What about Bart?"

"He's been waiting every day," said George, hopping on his bike. "But today I'm stopping at the bike store so I won't get home until later."

"I bet Bart will be waiting anyway," said Lester as George spun off.

George pulled into Manny's Cycle Center. Manny was opening a delivery of new tires. George breathed in the smell of rubber. "I was wondering if you have any colored bike spokes," he said.

"'Fraid n't," said Manny, swallowing his vowels. He was Irish and spoke with an accent that George liked.

"Thanks anyway," said George. "I think I'll just have a look around." He wandered up and down the aisles eyeing the cycling accessories—lights, water bottles, fenders, rain gear. Fifteen minutes later he looked at his watch and started home.

When George got there, Bart wasn't waiting on the porch steps.

"Hey, where's Bart?" George asked.

"He came out 8 minutes ago," said George's mother. "But three minutes later, he spotted a mole and ran after it."

George whistled and Bart came running.

"Thinking about moles instead of me," said George. He gave Bart a pat, then followed his mother into the kitchen.

George took a swipe at a bowl of icing with his finger.

"George," scolded his mother without even turning around. George guessed that Lester was right. Mothers had eyes in the back of their heads too.

George went up to his room and looked at his logbook. During the first week of his experiment with Bart he had varied his routine every day, sometimes coming home earlier, sometimes later, occasionally at the usual time. He'd been careful to check his watch and record the time when he'd actually set off for home. So far Bart had gone out to the steps within minutes of his arrival. It seemed perfectly obvious to George that Bart knew when he was coming home, but how that worked was less clear.

George went downstairs to the back door, where Bart was waiting for a walk.

"Ssh," whispered Vivien. She was crouched down, her big blueberry eyes drilling into Boots the cat, who was asleep on the chair.

"What are you doing?" asked George.

Vivien put her finger to her lips. "I'm seeing if Boots will wake up if I stare at her," she whispered. "Just like you said."

Boots's ears wiggled several times, but she didn't wake up. Vivien sighed. "Maybe Boots and I aren't connected," she said.

"You don't even know what that means," said George.

Vivien stood up, took a step backward, and put her hands on her hips. "What does it mean?" she asked.

What did it mean? George had to think about that. "Being connected means knowing how someone else feels or thinks," he said at last.

Vivien looked relieved. "Well, I know how Boots feels,"

she said. "And Boots knows how I feel. Or else she wouldn't come to me when I'm sad."

"See? Then you're connected," said George. "You don't need to prove it with an experiment."

"Then why are you always proving things with experiments?" asked Vivien.

George shrugged. He didn't really know. Why did people do experiments, anyway? He guessed that science and experiments were there to find out what was true, or at least what was more true than wasn't, because even things that people knew to be true sometimes changed, like when people thought the world was flat and then found out it was round.

That evening after dinner, Mr. Masson brought up the caterpillars. "It looks like it's caterpillar time," he said. "And you know what that means?"

George did know. Each spring when the caterpillars left their nests they would crawl along the cement foundation of the house. There were hundreds of them. And if they weren't stopped they would begin to eat the greenery. So George's father paid the children to pick them off the foundation and collect them in coffee cans.

"I've upped the ante this year," said Mr. Masson. "I'm paying a nickel per caterpillar."

"Wow," said Vivien, impressed. "Can we invite friends?"

"The more the merrier," said Mr. Masson.

George's mother followed George up to his room with a clothes basket. She opened his dresser and stacked a pile of T-shirts in the drawer.

"Do your homework," she said to George.

"How do you know it's not already done?" said George.

His mother raised her eyebrows and gave George one of her knowing looks.

George closed the dictionary and took out his homework. Maybe George couldn't prove that mothers had eyes in back of their heads, but they sure seemed to know what was going on.

Dear Dr. Sheldrake,

First I'd like you to know that my experiment with Bart, my dog, is going very well and I'm keeping a logbook. I know you do some experiments on staring. They seem really fun and I'd like to ask you something about them. I think people in some professions develop telepathy. Like teachers and maybe mothers. They always seem to know what's going on. It's like they have eyes in back of their head. Have you ever done any experiments with teachers or mothers?

Sincerely,
George Masson

Dear George,

Lots of people can tell when they're being looked at from behind. Most people have had this experience, as I think you'll discover if you ask your friends and members of your family. Surveys conducted in the state of Ohio showed that more than 90 percent of both grownups and children often had this experience. So there does seem to be a way in which we can feel when people are looking at us.

I've done many experiments to test this and it seems that many people really do have "eyes in back of their head." Some people can even detect when they are being watched through a closed-circuit TV system.

I think teachers can feel what's happening behind them because they develop this sensitivity through practice, and they may be better at it than people who don't have to stand at the front of classrooms. It would be interesting to set up a test comparing the sensitivity of teachers with that of other grownups who are not teachers. As far as I know no one has done this yet.

Certainly in the animal kingdom mothers seem to be able to influence their children by some degree of telepathy. There is a wonderful study of foxes by a great American naturalist named William Long who wrote a book called *How Animals Talk*. In it, he describes how a vixen, a mother fox, controls her young just by her look. If one is getting too far away or playing too boisterously she just looks at him and "the eager cub suddenly checks himself, turns as if he had heard a command, catches the vixen's look, and back he comes like a trained dog to the whistle."

If you are interested in reading more about how animals communicate, I think you'd enjoy William Long's book.

Best wishes,
Rupert Sheldrake

13

After school on Wednesday, Lester left the schoolyard and turned onto Cherry Street. He'd decided to kill time by wandering around the neighborhood before heading home. On Monday he'd taken a longer route, but Bill Gates had still gone out to the gate within minutes of his leaving school. On Tuesday Lester had ridden his bike and left school at 3 p.m. sharp, racing home as fast as he could. Bill Gates had been waiting 9 minutes—the exact time it had taken Lester to bike home.

Lester had noticed that a lot of the streets in his new neighborhood were named after fruits, or had something to do with them. He lived on Fig Street, but there was a Grove, Plum, and Orchard too. There was a playground on Orchard Street and Lester stopped and plopped himself into the bucket of one of the swings. Then he pumped high into the air and let go. He liked flying through the air. It made him feel like a bird.

Lester climbed the slide and threw himself down several times, once headfirst. Then he stopped to watch a group of kids playing tag, wondering if they might ask him to join them. But no one did.

Lester walked across a wide expanse of green grass hemmed in by a bike path.

"Bill Gates would love this," he said out loud.

Lester sat down on a park bench. A whirlybird floated down from a maple tree above him. Lester opened its pod and felt the sticky stuff inside. It looked like mayonnaise. Lester leaned back and watched the world go by. Then he heard someone shout, "Isn't that the fat guy with the mustard?"

Who, me? thought Lester glancing around. Two guys whizzed past on skateboards.

"I hate mustard," said one of them.

"It stinks," said the other.

"Hey," cried Lester. "It doesn't stink as much as the marsh."

Lester stood up. He was ready to go home. He realized that he hadn't been repeating his mantra. "Moving is fun. Change can be positive," he said halfheartedly.

Bill Gates was waiting on the walkway when Lester arrived.

"He's been there for 7 minutes," said Lester's mother, grinning widely. Lester looked at his watch. It had taken him 12 minutes to walk from the park home.

"Come on, big guy," said Lester. "Let's go for a walk. I found the perfect place. Almost," he added, remembering the skateboarders.

Lester led Bill Gates toward the park. Bill Gates stopped once to sniff some weeds growing along the sidewalk and a second time to bark at a squirrel. Then he trotted on. When they got to the park Lester tossed a stick into the wide sea of green grass and Bill Gates bounded after it.

"Hey, you," cried a groundsman. "No dogs allowed on the green. Get your mutt off there."

"Is he talking to us?" said Lester, corralling Bill Gates. He looked around. There was no one on the green but them and the groundsman, who was strolling their way. He nodded stiffly.

"Can you imagine what this green would look like if everyone let their dogs on it?" he said.

Lester could imagine. It would look like the green in his neighborhood in Denver—a big patch of blotched grass and a lot of people and dogs having fun.

"I don't make the rules," said the groundsman. He reached down and gave Bill Gates a pat.

At least he's friendly, thought Lester.

"Sorry," said Lester.

"I'm sorry too," said the groundsman.

They started home. "You can't do much here, can you?" said Lester. He repeated his mantra a few more times. "Moving is fun. Change can be positive." Halfway home he stopped to pet Bill Gates.

"Don't worry about the green," he said out loud. "Everyone makes mistakes." At least people in Denver made mistakes. He wondered if maybe people from Cape Cod didn't.

Lester followed the maze of streets back to Fig, where he turned into his driveway, which ran alongside the house. His father had just gotten in from a run. "They have some fantastic trails for jogging here," he said.

"Maybe," said Lester. "But you're not allowed on the public grass."

"That's a shame," said Mr. Shoe. Then he added, "But the rules are different in every state, and in every town. And I guess we have to respect them, don't we?"

"I guess," said Lester.

Lester and his father went into the kitchen. "I bet you didn't know that it's against the law to spit on the ground in some states," his father said. He opened the refrigerator and downed a fruit smoothie.

Lester shook his head. He didn't know that. "I think they're all ketchup guys here," he said.

"Ketchup guys?" said his father, looking puzzled. "What do you mean?"

"No one here likes mustard," said Lester.

"I believe mustard's an acquired taste," said Mr. Shoe. "I'd check back with them in a few months' time."

Lester sighed. He wondered if Cape Cod was an acquired taste.

Lester rested his eyes on a mound of oatmeal cookies on a white porcelain plate on the kitchen counter. Ordinarily they would have set his mouth watering and he would have dived in. But now he wasn't very hungry. He still had that empty feeling that gnawed away at his insides. But he wasn't craving food. He was craving Denver.

Bill Gates hovered around his water bowl and food dish. He didn't seem hungry either.

Lester went upstairs and filled in his logbook. "You know when I'm coming home, buddy, don't you?" he said. "There's just one problem. This doesn't feel like home." Lester sighed. "I miss Denver."

That night Lester lay in bed and cried for the first time since he'd moved to Cape Cod. He felt the tears stream down his face, big bubbles of loneliness, of missing all the things that were familiar. "Maybe I am a little overweight," he said to Bill Gates. "And maybe you have some mutt in you. But that didn't bother anyone in Denver."

Lester dropped his head into Bill Gates's fur. It felt soft and warm. "I just want to go back to my real home," he said. "Denver."

Lester closed his eyes and fell into a deep sleep. He dreamed he was a bird, swooping and soaring in and among the clouds. Beneath him was Denver and the green, burnished from wear and tear, where he used to take Bill Gates for a walk. When Lester woke up in the morning he'd made a decision. He didn't know how that could happen in his sleep, but it had. He reached into his desk drawer and took out the wad of money he'd been saving for an aquarium.

"We're going back to Denver," he said to Bill Gates. He didn't think about what he'd do when he got there. He didn't really care.

14

The next day after school Lester stopped at the bus station before going home.

"I'd like a ticket to Denver," he said to the woman at the window. "For Saturday morning."

"How old are you?" asked the woman.

"Almost eleven," said Lester.

The woman shook her head. "You have to be sixteen or traveling with someone who is sixteen or older."

"I'm traveling with Bill Gates," said Lester.

"Bill Gates?" said the woman, raising an eyebrow.

"He's a dog and he's seven," said Lester, nodding. "But in dog years that's at least forty, so he's an adult."

"Sorry, young man," said the woman. "I can't sell you a ticket."

"She didn't have to rub it in by calling me young," Lester said to Bill Gates when he got home. Bill Gates had been waiting 14 minutes for Lester's arrival, three minutes less than the time it had taken Lester to walk from the bus station to his house. Lester opened his logbook and recorded his data. Then he closed it and opened his notebook. His eyes skimmed his list of virtues. He'd checked off a few but there were plenty left. He obviously hadn't given the mantra enough time to unleash them.

"I guess we'll just have to go on foot," said Lester, scratching Bill Gates under the chin. "It might take days, or even weeks." Lester stopped himself before he got to months. "There are tons of stories about dogs who find their way back home over thousands of miles. If they can do it, you can do it." Lester rubbed Bill Gates's back. "And we can lose weight too," he added. "That's what they call killing two birds with one stone."

Lester followed Bill Gates into the backyard. Above him a swarm of birds soared across the sky, dipping and turning in perfect unison.

"They're returning from their winter home," said Lester's mother, who was filling a bird feeder hanging from a tree.

"So I guess they have two homes," said Lester. "One in the north and one in the south." He reflected on how Denver was west and Cape Cod was east. But he didn't take that thought any further.

Lester went up to his room and stuffed a change of clothing into a backpack, along with a map, his travel toothbrush and toothpaste, a pack of Bill Gates's favorite biscuits, and his notebook. "This is good practice," he said to Bill Gates. "Just taking the things you need. You really don't need too much," he added. Then he rolled up his sleeping bag and his pup tent and strapped them to his backpack. The last thing he took was his house key, which was attached to a key chain with a rubber frog.

Suddenly, Lester was reminded of a book he'd had when he was little. It was called *A Boy, a Dog, a Frog, and a Friend*. He was a boy, Bill Gates was a dog. And there was a frog on the end of his key chain. The only thing missing was a friend.

15

Bill Gates was waiting on the walkway when Lester arrived home from school on his bike. It was Friday, day 9 of his experiment.

"He's been there 10 minutes," said Lester's mother. She was standing on a ladder with a brush, putting the finishing touches on her studio. She'd painted it a bright sunny yellow.

Lester leaned down and nuzzled Bill Gates's nose. "I know what you're waiting for," he said softly. "You're waiting to go to Denver. Me too. But you have to wait until tomorrow. Hey," said Lester to his mother. "I thought you were painting your studio blue."

Lester's mother smiled. "I thought so too," she said. "But I had a change of heart."

Lester stood in the middle of the freshly painted room. Sunshine poured through the window like a spotlight, bathing him in a golden halo.

"Maybe I could paint my room yellow," he said aloud. Then he added quietly, "If I weren't going to Denver, which I am. Right, Bill Gates?"

Bill Gates got to his feet and followed Lester into the kitchen.

"What's up?" chirped Carlos.

"Lester wants a cracker," said Lester, reaching into the cupboard. He prepared himself a snack—crackers spread with almond butter and a tall glass of milk. Then he leaned down and looked at the world upside down for a few seconds. The room seemed strange. It reminded Lester of something his father had once said. "Things appear different depending on how you look at them." Lester righted his head. He preferred the view from that angle. He guessed that was because he was used to it.

"Probably if I stood on my head for a week, then I'd get used to the way things looked that way too," he said to Bill Gates.

Lester filled in his logbook, then started down Chestnut Street, Bill Gates in tow. "There must be some chestnut trees around here," he said, "or they wouldn't have named it that."

Lester looked upward. A bird was building a nest on a branch in a tree overhead.

"I bet she's going to lay some eggs," said Lester. "But we won't be here to see them. We'll be in Denver." Lester gave Bill Gates a reassuring pat. "But birds hatch eggs there too. Hey, that's something these two places have in common."

Lester turned the corner onto Acorn Street. "Chestnuts, acorns," he said. "More nuts." He slowed down next to a van parked along the side of the road. It had pastel cupcakes, tarts, pies, and cakes with candles painted on one side.

"Yum," said Lester.

A little girl poked her head out from behind the van. "Hi," she said. "I'm Vivien."

"Hi," said Lester, peering into the window of the van. "Is it your birthday or something?" he asked.

"No," said Vivien. "That's my mom's delivery van. She's a pastry chef."

"Jeez," said Lester. "You're lucky."

"You too," said Vivien, turning to Bill Gates. "You have such a cute dog. Can I pet him?"

"Sure," said Lester. "He loves attention."

"I love dogs," said Vivien. "What's your dog's name?"

"Bill Gates," said Lester.

Suddenly George appeared. "Hey, Lester," he said. "What's up?"

"I'm taking Bill Gates for a walk," said Lester. "Where's Bart?"

"Napping," said George.

"Oh, so you must be the new boy in George's class," said Vivien. "The one who came from that place with the long street." She picked up her jump rope and began to swing it in circles. "Why did you name your dog Bill Gates?" she asked.

"I wanted to name him after a great man who changed our lives," said Lester. "And that's Bill Gates."

"I wonder if Bill Gates knows there's a dog named after him," said Vivien.

Lester shrugged.

"You could write and tell him," said Vivien. "George writes to famous people all the time, don't you?" Vivien looked at George.

"Not really," said George.

"You wrote to that Rupert Sheldrake person," said Vivien.

"He's nowhere near as famous as Bill Gates," said George.

"Did he write you back?" asked Lester.

George nodded.

Lester looked impressed. "Maybe I will write to Bill Gates," he said. His eyes traveled up the walkway to the front porch. "I used to have a porch just like that. In Denver," he said, his eyes becoming watery. George noticed that they were greenish-blue, just like the cordgrass on the marsh. Lester continued. "Bill Gates misses Denver," he said. "He had a lot of nice friends there."

"We have lots of nice dogs here too," said Vivien. "And people," she added, crossing her arms and hopping through the loop she'd made with the rope. "We're nice, aren't we, George?"

"I guess so," said George, leaning over to pet Bill Gates. He was feeling a little uncomfortable. Maybe he hadn't been as nice to Lester as he could have been.

"Do you want to come and collect caterpillars with us tomorrow?" asked Viven. "This year we get a nickel apiece for each one. We put them in coffee cans and my dad takes them to caterpillar city."

"Caterpillar city?" said Lester. "Where's that?" He guessed it must be somewhere on Cape Cod.

Vivien was thoughtful. "I don't know," she shrugged. "It's somewhere, though."

"Well," said Lester, remembering his trip to Denver. "I think I might be going away. But if I'm here, sure, I'll come."

"If you're here," said Vivien, "we're starting at around ten."

George had never invited anyone to collect caterpillars before, except for Kyra. And he had never told anyone but her what happened to them. The truth was that his father burned them, and George hated the thought of it.

"Why did you ask Lester to come collect caterpillars?" George asked Vivien after Lester and Bill Gates had left.

"Because Dad said we could invite anyone we wanted," said Vivien. "And I wanted to ask Lester." She picked up her jump rope and started jumping again. "Don't you think Bill Gates looks like Lester?" she said.

"Maybe," said George. They were both kind of disheveled and messy-looking. "Do you think I look like Bart?"

Vivien stopped jumping long enough to look at Bart, then back at George. "No," she said. She sounded pretty sure. Then she asked, "Why don't you like Lester?"

"Who said I don't like Lester?" said George.

"It just seems like you don't," said Vivien.

George was relieved to be interrupted by the huffing and puffing of Mr. Alvaros, their next-door neighbor, wobbling past, overloaded with grocery bags.

"I'll get those for you," said George, offering Mr. Alvaros a hand. He took two of the bags.

"Thank you, son," said Mr. Alvaros, patting George on the cheek. His hand was dry and cool.

"I can help too," said Vivien.

"Bless your soul, Vivien," said Mr. Alvaros, handing Vivien a canvas handbag.

George and Vivien left the groceries in Mr. Alvaros's entranceway and headed back down the walkway.

"Why did he call you son?" asked Vivien. "You're not his son."

"It's just a figure of speech," said George.

"What's that?" asked Vivien.

"An expression," said George.

Then Vivien asked, "What's a soul?"

George frowned. He had wondered the same thing, but he didn't want to admit he didn't have a good answer.

"It's the part of you that you can't see," said George. Vivien sat down on the front steps and dropped her chin into her hands. She looked down at herself, puzzled, and then back at George. George tried again. It was a hard question.

"It's the part that feels," he said at last.

"Oh," said Vivien. "Does everyone have one?"

"I think so," said George. Vivien looked relieved.

"Does Bart have a soul?" asked Vivien.

"Sure," said George. He thought Bart must have a soul. All of a sudden he wondered if caterpillars had souls. He guessed they probably did.

Meanwhile, Lester wove back through the streets of nuts. He couldn't stop thinking about caterpillar city, wondering where it was and what it was like. There were caterpillars in Denver but he'd never heard of a city named after them.

"If you want," he said to Bill Gates, "we could postpone our trip to Denver half a day. Then we could collect caterpillars with George and Vivien. It might be fun."

When Lester arrived home, Carlos was sitting on the window ledge. "What's up?" he chirped.

Lester looked out the open window into the backyard. His neighbor Mrs. Robarts had just closed the door of her toolshed and was hurrying back to her house.

16

"Why don't I like Lester?" George asked himself that night. He stood before the bathroom mirror brushing his teeth. It wasn't really that he didn't like Lester. It was just that he felt that if he liked Lester then Lester would in some way be taking Kyra's place.

"And that place is sacred," George said. He wasn't really sure what that word meant, but he'd heard it on television and it sounded good. That reminded George that he'd heard Lester talking to himself out loud. He'd even seen him running around the schoolyard shouting "The sky is falling." Maybe that was weird. But George was weird too sometimes. He got compulsions to do things that other people might think were strange, like spinning like a top.

George climbed into bed and checked the clock. At exactly 9 p.m. he began to think of a fruit. It was a game he sometimes played with Kyra—another experiment, really. Before falling asleep, one of them would think of a fruit for ten minutes, and the other would have to guess which fruit it was. Tonight it was George's turn to guess what fruit Kyra was thinking about. George waited, but nothing came to mind. Finally he texted "purple grapes." He waited for Kyra to text back. "Lime," she wrote. He'd gotten it wrong. George took a deep breath and exhaled loudly. Sometimes it worked and sometimes it didn't. Sometimes he felt he was totally connected and that he had a clear and present line right through to Kyra. Then other times he couldn't capture that feeling. George wondered why he couldn't will it. How much depended on him and how much on Kyra? And how much on things that were completely beyond his control? Maybe it was some combination of things.

"Tomorrow's caterpillar day," texted George. "We invited Lester."

Kyra texted back. "That was nice of you," she wrote. "Say hi to him for me. And give his dog a pat."

"Sure," wrote George. But he was wishing Kyra were there to do those things herself.

George looked out the window and into the sky, at the stars, pulsating as though they were breathing. He linked them with his eyes as if they were dot-to-dots. The Big Dipper was right above him. It occurred to him that maybe he was connected to Kyra in the same way the stars were connected, in some sort of invisible design. Despite the distance, he knew it was true. So why did he have to do experiments? Weren't there some things people just knew? As George looked up at the sky, he knew he was looking at some strange place where science and spirit met. And even though he was outside of that space he knew that he was part of it. What was "spirit," anyway? One of those funny words like "soul," which was hard to define. That part of himself that he got a glimpse of every so often. It was that part of him that knew how others felt. The part of him that knew how he felt. It was the part of him that knew full well that it was not Lester's fault that Kyra had moved. It was just life. And things happened in life. And you didn't like all of them.

George sighed. He wished he could think of an experiment to prove that there was a soul.

Dear Dr. Sheldrake,

I live on Cape Cod and I'm doing an experiment with my best friend, Kyra, who moved to North Carolina. One of us thinks about a fruit from a list for ten minutes. And the other one tries to guess which fruit it is. My friend Kyra almost always gets it right so I guess she must be telepathic. How do you think that works? Do you think it's the same telepathy as dogs who know when their owners are coming home?

Sincerely,
George Masson

P.S. North Carolina is about 750 miles from Cape Cod, in case you don't know.

Dear George,

I'm glad you're trying this out with Kyra and I think it's a good experiment. The only thing is you should make sure that the fruit you think of is selected at random. Otherwise, Kyra might be getting it right just by figuring out what you're going to think of next. For example, if you thought of an apple yesterday, today she might think, "Oh, it won't be an apple because George did that yesterday." So you should do it using a real random selection method. The easiest would be to write the names of fruits on slips of paper, mix them thoroughly, and pick one from a hat or a bowl.

Telepathy happens between people or animals that are closely bonded to each other. It happens with animals that are members of the same group, like wolves in a pack, or between animals that are very attached to a particular person, like between your dog and you, or between people who are good friends or members of the same family. "Tele" is a Greek word meaning distant, as in telephone or television, and "path" is a Greek word meaning feeling, as in sympathy or empathy. So telepathy is mainly about feelings, picking up on what another person needs, what they are doing, or what their intentions are. Bart seems to be picking up on your intention to come home and responding to that. Animals and people may also be able to respond to thoughts or pictures in our minds, and that seems to be what Kyra is doing.

Don't forget to record the results of your experiment and let me know how you get on.

Best wishes,
Rupert Sheldrake

17

On Saturday morning Lester pedaled into the Massons' driveway and pulled to a stop alongside Mrs. Masson's pastry van. He'd decided to postpone his trip to Denver for a few hours. That way he could see caterpillar city.

"Hey, Lester. I thought you couldn't come," cried Vivien, running out to greet him.

"I had a change of heart," said Lester. He liked that expression, the way it referred to a feeling, a fluttering, somewhere deep in his chest. He'd felt it when he awoke that morning and thought about going to Denver.

"Great," said Vivien. She skipped back to the steps where she'd been making mud pies, flat pats of wet earth sprinkled with teaberries and leaves. "Want a mud pie?" she asked, holding out a plate.

"Thanks," said Lester, taking the plate politely and

going through the motions of eating. Lester rubbed his belly. "Yummm. I love pie. Maybe I can try one of your mother's."

"Her lemon meringue is the best," said Vivien.

"I hope I'll have enough room for it after all that mud pie," said Lester, continuing to pat his belly.

Lester reached in his pocket and took out a bird whistle. He blew it loudly.

"That's lovely," said Vivien. "What is it?"

"It's to call nightingales," said Lester. "You want to try?" He held the whistle out to Vivien. She took it and looked at the end, wondering whether or not she should wipe it clean. She decided not to bother and put it directly to her lips and whistled.

"You can have it if you want," said Lester.

"Thanks," said Vivien. "But then how will you call nightingales?"

Lester twisted his lips into a knot and blew gently just like his father had shown him. The sound that came out was nearly the same as that of the whistle.

Vivien was impressed. "Where did you learn that?" she asked.

"My dad taught me," said Lester, remembering his first visit to Cape Cod, when his dad had patiently taught him to whistle like a nightingale. Lester had practiced for days on end and it had come to pass. Sort of like a mantra, Lester thought. That reminded him that he'd not been practicing his. Lester repeated it quietly. "Moving is fun. Change can be positive."

"What did you say?" asked Vivien.

"Oh, nothing," said Lester.

George came around from the back of the house where he'd been searching for sticks to coax the caterpillars off the cement foundation and into the coffee cans.

"Hi, Lester," he said. "I thought you couldn't come."

"I didn't want to miss caterpillar city," said Lester.

"Lester can whistle like a nightingale," said Vivien. "And he's going to teach me. Can you teach George too?"

"If he wants," said Lester.

"What about me?" said Zac playfully, ducking out of the garage. "I want to whistle like a bird."

"No you don't," said Vivien. She turned to Lester. "That's my brother Zac."

"Hi, Zac," said Lester.

"And this is Lester," said Vivien.

Zac high-fived Lester. "Like your colored spokes," he said, admiring Lester's bike. "I think George needs some of those."

George nodded. "I checked Manny's," he said. "But they didn't have any." Then he handed Lester a coffee can and a stick.

Lester tapped the stick gently against the side of the can. Then he followed George around to the back of the house. The foundation was crawling with fuzzy caterpillars with yellow and brown flecks.

George began prying the caterpillars off the wall with his stick, watching their bodies tighten, coil, then give way as he shook them into the coffee can. He worked fast, getting as many as he could in case they got any ideas about crawling back out. But somehow they didn't. George had a sinking feeling in the pit of his stomach. He wondered how the caterpillars felt, if they knew what they were in for. Every year George hoped for some intelligence to change the pattern so they wouldn't return. But it didn't happen.

Lester's voice rose and fell in the background. "Hey, little bugger," he said. "Come on over here. Where do you think you're going, fuzzy-wuzzy? Whoops, there you go. Two at a time."

Vivien set down her coffee can and stick and blew into the bird whistle. Then she asked, "Where's caterpillar city? Lester wants to visit it."

George fidgeted uncomfortably. "It's somewhere near the dump," he said, lying.

George was glad when his father appeared dressed in his yard clothes—a faded corduroy shirt, a pair of stained khakis, canvas sneakers, and a fishing hat.

"How's it going, everyone?" he asked.

"Great," said Vivien. She went back to work, winding her stick around the caterpillars, shaking them into the can. "Caterpillar city must be beautiful when the caterpillars turn into butterflies," she said. "I'd like to visit it too."

George pursed his lips. "I'm not sure that's a good idea," he said. "Because we might scare them off." George looked at Lester—one of those knowing looks that spoke of truth. Lester seemed to understand.

"Maybe it's not such a good idea after all," he said. "I wouldn't want to risk scaring them."

"Me neither," said Vivien with a frown.

Mr. Masson stretched a hand toward Lester. "Who's this young man?" he asked.

"Lester," said George. "He's just moved here from Denver."

Lester wiped a hand on the leg of his pants and offered it to Mr. Masson. "Hi," he said.

"So, Lester," said Mr. Masson. "This must be a big change for you."

Lester nodded. "Denver's a lot different," he said.

Vivien spoke, interrupting them. "Do you think the caterpillars know they are going to the city? I'll bet the other caterpillars are waiting for them. Don't you, George?"

"Yup," said George, feeling his stomach turn.

When they'd picked every last caterpillar off the wall, Mr. Masson checked to see that the lids were sealed and he set the cans in the garage.

"I got fifty," said Vivien. "That makes two dollars and fifty cents."

"Bravo," said Zac. "What are you going to do with it?"

"George is taking me to the fair," said Vivien.

"I am?" said George. He'd forgotten that he'd promised.

"Yes," said Vivien. "This afternoon." Vivien placed a hand on Lester's forearm. "Do you want to come with us?" she asked.

"I can't," Lester said. "I still have to go somewhere this afternoon."

"That's too bad," said Vivien.

It is too bad, thought Lester. It would have been fun to go to the fair. But he was leaving for Denver.

"What are you going to do with your money?" Vivien asked him.

"I'm saving up for an aquarium," said Lester.

Vivien wrinkled her nose. "You must like fish," she said. "I think they're slimy. But George loves them, don't you, George?" Vivien turned to her brother. "George loves all animals," she said. Then she furrowed her brow. "Are fish animals?"

"Close enough," said George

"What about you, George?" asked Zac. "What are you going to do with your money?"

"I think I'll just save it," said George.

"George never spends anything," said Vivien. "He must have a million dollars by now."

George rolled his eyes. "That's not true," he said.

"Well, almost," said Vivien.

Lester hopped onto his bike. "I better go," he said.

"Thanks." He was about to say see you later, but then he remembered that he was going to Denver.

Meanwhile, George went into the house wishing and wondering. Wishing that he was going to caterpillar city with Vivien rather than the fair. And wondering if spring would ever come without the caterpillars.

Dear Dr. Sheldrake,

This question isn't really about dogs or telepathy but it's about animals so I hope you will answer it. Each year the caterpillars return to our house and climb on the foundation. There are hundreds of them. And each year we peel them off, put them in coffee cans, and burn them. But each year they come back again. Do you think this will ever change? Do you think they will ever learn not to come back?

Yours truly,

George Masson

Dear George,

When I was a child I used to collect caterpillars and watch them pupate and turn into butterflies. But here in England we don't have caterpillars that climb up houses so I've never actually seen this. Obviously the ones that get burned are not going to come back, but a new generation the next year climb up and fix themselves on the wall because it's their instinct to do so. It's an inherited behavioral pattern. And lots of them do it on trees or rocks, I suppose, because they must have been doing this long before people started building houses. Old instincts like this are hard to change. Also, insects don't learn very much, and I doubt they will stop doing it just because so many got killed the year before.

I certainly wish insects would learn. In the summer when I'm plagued by mosquitos, I kill them because I hate being bitten. But however many I kill, more keep coming. I suppose lots of other people do the same thing, and mosquitoes still keep trying to suck their blood. The fact is a lot of them succeed, and if they didn't suck blood they would die out. That's why animals need instincts, because it's how they survive. Even if lots of them get killed, enough survive to carry on breeding the next year.

Best wishes,
Rupert Sheldrake

18

When Lester got home from the Massons' he sat down to lunch—one of his favorites, chicken noodle soup with rye crisps. It actually tasted better because he knew it might be his last Cape Cod lunch for a while. That was strange.

After lunch Lester strolled into the backyard. Bill Gates was lapping up the midday sun. He looked content, maybe because he knew it might be the last time in a while that he'd be soaking up the Cape Cod sun. Lester wondered why people enjoyed things more when they knew they might not do them again. He knew the answer. It was because they were living in the present. Why couldn't people always live in the present? Lester asked himself. But the answer to that was harder.

Lester's father was in the garden studying a stubby tree dwarfed by its larger neighbors. He was neatly dressed in his yard clothes, a flannel shirt and over-alls.

"I'm taking Bill Gates for a long walk," said Lester. "Goodbye." He said the word with emotion, but his father didn't seem to notice.

"Hmm," grunted Mr. Shoe, who had gotten down on his hands and knees and begun sprinkling fertilizer around the roots of the stubby tree. "What the devil ails you?" he said.

For a brief moment, Lester felt a funny connection to the tree, a feeling of not being understood. "I bet if you talk to it nicely, it might start growing," he said. He walked over to the tree and petted it just like he might Bill Gates. "There's nothing wrong with you," he said. "You are a lovely, lovely tree." Then he turned to Bill Gates. "Come on."

Lester passed through the kitchen one last time. "Goodbye," he said to Carlos.

"Goodbye, dear Lester," said Carlos.

"Hey, when did you learn the word 'dear'?" asked Lester.

Lester's mother was sitting cross-legged on a mat in her studio, deep in meditation. The scent of a lit candle wafted Lester's way. He thought it smelled like sunshine, or how he imagined sunshine would smell.

"Goodbye," he said. "I'm taking Bill Gates on a long, long walk."

Lester's mother nodded, but she didn't come out of her trance, nor open her eyes.

"They might not even notice we're gone," said Lester. He gathered up his backpack and headed for the door.

"Bye, house," he said, stopping before the faded cape. The shades waved gracefully as if to say goodbye. But suddenly Lester realized that he'd never really said hello.

19

Vivien clutched her money in her fist. "I'm going into the haunted house," she said to George. "Want to come with me?"

George shook his head. "I think I'll stay here," he said.

"I'll buy you a ticket if you want to come," said Vivien.

"I don't really want to," said George.

"Too bad Lester isn't here," said Vivien. "You could have done something with him."

George agreed. "I bet he would have liked the Flying Saucer," he said. The Flying Saucer was a ride that sent you hurtling skyward while spinning in a circle. It made George feel like he was going into space.

Vivien puckered her mouth and squeezed her fist tighter.

"Are you scared?" George asked. He didn't think there was anything frightening about the haunted house— not if you were eleven, anyway. But Vivien was only eight. George couldn't really remember what eight felt like.

"I'm not scared," said Vivien, mustering all her courage.

"I'll wait for you at the exit," said George.

George watched Vivien climb the stairs of rattling bones and blinking lights. Every two or three steps she would look back at George with anticipation, and George would feel forced to wave. When she'd disappeared inside, George wandered toward the exit. He passed a booth with a redheaded fortune-teller, stopping just long enough to ask himself if anyone's hair could really be that color. The woman, who was holding a deck of cards, beckoned to George with a purple fingernail.

George didn't really believe in fortunes. Besides, they cost two dollars and fifty cents. He walked on, but after several steps he felt a mysterious pull propelling him toward the lady with the red hair and purple fingernails. He turned, walked up to the fortune-teller, and put two dollars and fifty cents on the table.

"What's your name?" asked the woman.

"George," said George. "Masson," he added, "with two s's." He wanted to make sure she knew that in case it meant something.

"So," she said. She took George's left hand in her palm and studied it. Then she told George that he was particularly intelligent and that he would have a long life. George smiled to himself. He bet she told that to everyone.

The fortune-teller paused for a few seconds. "I see you have an affinity for animals," she said.

George wasn't sure about the meaning of affinity, but he guessed it meant that he liked them. He wondered how she could know that. Maybe he smelled like dog or had some hairs on his clothing. Maybe he looked like a pet lover. Or maybe she had some sixth sense that enabled her to read his mind. The thought was a little creepy.

The fortune-teller looked from George's hand into his eyes. "You, young man, will make an amazing discovery," she said.

"Like what?" asked George. "And when?" Did she mean in a few days or a few years? There was a big difference.

The fortune-teller shook her head. "That I don't know," she said.

George backed away slowly, disappointed. Then he turned toward the exit of the haunted house just as Vivien was being delivered in a cart.

"How was it?" asked George.

"It was scar-y," said Vivien. "Look, my hair is standing on end." She pulled the ends of her hair into the air and tugged on them.

"I had my fortune told," said George.

"Oh," said Vivien. "What did the lady say?"

"That I'd live a long life and I'd make an amazing discovery," said George.

"That's nice," said Vivien.

"I'm sure she says that to everyone," said George.

"Probably," said Vivien. She was quiet for a few moments. Then she pursed her lips and said, "You lied to me, George."

"What did I lie about?" asked George, puzzled.

"About the caterpillars," said Vivien, crossing her arms. "There is no such place as caterpillar city."

Now it was George's turn to say "Oh." He felt like a sword had been run through his heart.

"Dad burns them," said Vivien.

"How'd you find out?" asked George.

"I heard him talking about it with Zac," said Vivien.

"That's what you get for spying," said George. Vivien had a habit of spying on people. She called it "watching," but it was spying.

"I wasn't spying," said Vivien. "I was only listening."

"It's just that I didn't want to make you cry," said George.

"I wouldn't have cried," said Vivien. "Do you think I'm a baby?"

"Well, I might have cried," said George. "Do you think I like the thought of burning all those caterpillars and wondering if they know what's happening?"

Vivien's silence bored a hole into George's stomach. "I'm hungry," he said. "Let's get something to eat."

20

Lester and Bill Gates started off down the streets named after trees. Bill Gates trotted ahead as if he knew right where he was going. And Lester followed.

"I'm counting on you to get us out of town," said Lester. "Then we can hitchhike." Lester passed a store window and stopped to look at his reflection. He'd put on a fresh change of clothes, remembered his belt, and combed his hair. "We look nice," he said. "Someone is bound to pick us up."

As they continued on, Lester began to see things he hadn't noticed before. Up ahead was a small park with an agility course for dogs.

"Hey, look," Lester said to Bill Gates. "A dog gym." Bill Gates paused and then trotted on. A few streets farther, there was a miniature golf course like the one in Denver. "I didn't know they had mini golf here," said Lester. He loved mini golf.

Lester and Bill Gates wound in and out of the labyrinth of streets until one street began to look like the other.

"Denver might have the longest street," said Lester, stopping to catch his breath. "But this town must have the most of them." Without even thinking, he began repeating his mantra. "Moving is fun," he said. "Change can be positive."

Bill Gates rounded the block, picking up his pace.

"Slow down," cried Lester.

Next thing Lester knew he was standing before an agility course for dogs. "Another one?" he said. Then he realized it was the same course he'd seen earlier.

"What happened?" cried Lester. "We've been going around in circles. I thought you were taking us home." It occurred to Lester that he hadn't said Denver. Maybe Bill Gates thought of Cape Cod as home.

"This isn't home," Lester said to Bill Gates.

Bill Gates looked at Lester as if to say, "Isn't it?" Then he lowered his eyes.

"Denver is home," said Lester. His stomach had begun to growl. "All this exercise is making me hungry." He squinted into the distance. Not far ahead was a hot dog shop. Lester's mouth began to water. "I need something to eat," he said, crossing the street.

Lester parked Bill Gates outside and entered the hot dog shop. He took off his backpack and climbed onto one of the leather stools lining a long thin counter. Then he spun himself around until he began to feel dizzy.

"What's it going to be, son?" said the waiter.

"I'd like a hot dog with extra mustard," said Lester. "And a plain one for my dog." Lester gestured toward the window to Bill Gates, who was sitting back on his haunches waiting patiently.

Lester looked at the walls. They were covered with photos of dogs. "I like the decor," he said.

"Thanks," said the waiter. "The owner is a dog lover."

"Me too," said Lester.

The waiter smiled, then placed a steamy hot dog wrapped in a bun in front of Lester along with a bottle of mustard. Then he chopped a plain hot dog into a bowl for Bill Gates. Lester took a deep breath. He liked the smell of the place—a mix of hot dogs, soap bubbles, and fun. There were some game machines in a corner. They had some of those back in Denver.

Lester took the chopped hot dog out to Bill Gates. "Have I got a treat for you," he said. "Doesn't it smell de-lish?" Then he went back to his stool, picked up the bottle of mustard, and squirted a thick yellow stripe across the top of his hot dog. He took a bite. It was amazing. It may well have been the best hot dog Lester had ever tasted.

I wonder if it tastes so good because I'm so hungry, he thought. Or because it's my first Cape Cod hot dog. Or maybe my last.

Suddenly, the door to the shop swung open and in walked George and Vivien.

"Lester!" cried Vivien.

"George, Vivien," said Lester. "What are you doing here?"

"We were at the fair," said Vivien. "And George got hungry."

"These are the best hot dogs on Cape Cod," said George. He ordered one for himself and one for Vivien.

"They might be the best ones in the world," said Lester. Then it occurred to him that he hadn't seen all that much of the world. He'd spent most of his life in Denver.

"Don't you love the dog pictures?" said Vivien.

"Yup," said Lester.

George's hot dog arrived and he picked up the bottle of ketchup and gave it a squirt.

"You should try some mustard with that," said Lester. "Just a little."

"I've never really liked mustard," said George.

"But things change," said Lester, not really knowing why he said that. The idea of change had always troubled him. But now it didn't seem to—not that much, anyway. Lester wondered if maybe another virtue—Acceptance—had been unleashed without his even realizing it.

George picked up the mustard bottle and stared at it for a few seconds. At last he turned it upside down and squirted four small flecks onto his hot dog. Then he took a bite.

"How is it?" asked Vivien. She squirted a drop of mustard on her finger and licked it. "It stings," she said.

George swirled the hot dog around in his mouth, then swallowed the first bite. He took another and swallowed that too.

"Well?" said Lester.

"It's actually pretty good," said George.

"Are you going camping?" asked Vivien, eyeing Lester's backpack wedged between two stools.

"I am," said Lester.

"George loves camping," said Vivien. "Don't you, George?"

George nodded and took another bite of his hot dog. "Almost as much as I love hot dogs," he said.

"George camps in the backyard sometimes," said Vivien.

"Viven, would you please mind your own business," said George.

"I used to do that too, back in Denver," said Lester.

"Well, maybe we can do it here sometime," said George.

"That'd be fun," said Lester.

"We have to go," said Vivien, tugging on George's hand. "I have a playdate with my friend Madeleine. And," she added, "I'm spending the night."

"Sure," said Lester. "Have fun."

When Lester had finished his hot dog he went outside. "What are we going to do now?" he said to Bill Gates.

He looked left. Then he looked right. He felt as though he'd come to a crossroads.

"I wonder if you can have a change of heart more than once," he said to Bill Gates. Bill Gates dropped his chin as if to say, "Yes, that's what I've been trying to tell you."

Lester thought of the birds, of how they migrated every year. They had two homes. Maybe he could have two homes too. At least he could try.

"I guess we're going to have to go back with our tails between our legs," said Lester.

Bill Gates stood up and trotted off in the direction of 61 Fig Street, and Lester followed.

Lester's mother was in the kitchen making dinner, meat sauce and pasta. Its smell wafted through the house, making Lester's mouth water.

"Where have you been, Lester?" she cried. For once she wasn't smiling. "I was ready to call the police. You've been gone for hours."

"I told you I was taking Bill Gates on a long, long walk," said Lester. "Sorry," he added, but he was secretly happy that she'd noticed he was gone.

After dinner, Lester began setting up his tent in the backyard. "I think I'll sleep out tonight," he said to his father.

"Let me give you a hand," said Mr. Shoe, slipping a peg into a corner of the tent and thrusting it into the ground.

Lester rolled out his sleeping bag and lay down with Bill Gates curled up at his feet. Then before Lester knew it, his father had stretched out next to him.

"So how's it going?" he asked. "Are you feeling a little more at home here?"

Lester nodded. "Yeah," he said. "And I think Bill Gates is too."

From off in the distance came the cry of a gull. Lester listened closely, then tried to mimic the sound.

"It's like having to learn a new language, isn't it?" said his father.

Lester nodded in agreement. He was thinking how moving was like having to learn a language, but there was more to it than learning words. It was discovering how people acted and what things were like.

The gull cried one more time, a long, loud shriek.

This time Lester opened his mouth and let out a sound.

"I think you've got it," said his father.

"Maybe," said Lester, reaching out a toe to nuzzle Bill Gates, who'd fallen fast asleep. Not even the cries of the gull could rouse him. It had been a long day.

Lester repeated his mantra to himself quietly. "Moving is fun. Change can be positive." He was beginning to believe it.

21

On Monday afternoon George sat on a bench in front of the school waiting for Vivien. He had agreed to drop her at her dance class so that he could test Bart by arriving home much later than usual. He was now beginning the third week of his experiment.

Vivien skipped over to George and sat down next to him, lifting her feet into the air. "Do you like my new shoes?" she asked. They were blue ballerina-like slippers punched with silver sparkles along the strap.

George didn't like them. But he didn't not like them either. "If you like them, I like them," he said at last. That answer seemed to satisfy Vivien.

Suddenly a voice sounded from in back of them. "I come from the planet Xpos."

George turned around. It was Lester. He'd plucked a whirlybird from a tree, opened it, and stuck it across the bridge of his nose.

George smiled. He couldn't help but think that was

something that Kyra might have done. George looked down at his wrist at the green ribbon. It had begun to fray at the edges. "Hi, Lester," he said.

"Where's Xpos?" asked Vivien.

"I don't know," said Lester, tilting his head upward. "Somewhere out there." He sat down on the bench next to George. "Anyone want a whirlybird?" he asked.

"Sure," said George. "I'll take one."

Lester jumped up and grabbed one for George. George opened it and spread it across the bridge of his nose. Then Lester turned to Vivien and handed her a whirlybird too. "Here," he said.

Vivien wrinkled her nose and hesitated.

"Come on, Viv," said George. "It feels really funny."

Vivien opened the whirlybird and pressed it across the bridge of her nose. "It's sticky," she said.

Lester lifted his head skyward again. "Do you think there's life on other planets?" he asked.

George had often wondered the same thing. "Why not?" he said. "I mean, why would we be the only living beings in the universe?"

"Zac thinks George could be an alien," said Vivien.

Lester looked earnestly at George, the whirlybird still on his nose. George tried hard not to laugh. "Sometimes I feel like an alien," said Lester, his voice sounding nasal. "Especially since I moved here. Everything is so different than it was in Denver."

George thought about the marsh and how he loved

his life on Cape Cod—all of it. "I don't think I'd like to move," he said.

"Moving is fun," said Lester. "Change can be positive."

"What?" asked Vivien. She looked confused.

"That's my mantra," said Lester. He repeated it another time. "Moving is fun. Change can be positive."

"What's a mantra?" asked Vivien.

"Basically, it's a bunch of words you say a bunch of times until they come true," said Lester. Then he added, "Mantras can unleash virtues."

"What are those?" asked Vivien.

"They're good qualities about a person," said Lester. "You know, like friendliness, loyalty, patience, tolerance." Those were the first ones that came to Lester's mind.

"I've got some of those," said Vivien. "But I'd like a mantra to get even more." She swung her ballerina shoes into the air. "Happy all the time," she said. "That can be my mantra."

Lester climbed onto the bench and grabbed another whirlybird. He stuck a second one on his nose. Then he sat back down. Mrs. Robarts was walking by the schoolyard with a cart of groceries.

"Hey, that's my neighbor," whispered Lester. "Speaking of aliens, I think she could be hiding one. Actually, I think she might be a criminal."

"Why do you think that?" asked George.

"She's always sneaking out to the toolshed," said Lester. "And I hear her talking to someone."

Vivien's eyes grew bigger. "Do you think she kidnapped someone?" she asked.

"You should follow her," said George.

"Can we follow her too?" asked Vivien.

"Not today," said George. "You have to go to dance class, and I have to get home and see if Bart is waiting for me."

"Be careful," said Vivien when Lester got up to leave. She looked worried. "I wouldn't want you to be kidnapped."

"Don't worry," said Lester. Then he repeated Vivien's mantra. "Happy all the time," he said.

"Happy all the time," said Vivien, laughing.

When Lester got home, he found Bill Gates at the gate chewing on a dog bone.

"He's been there 25 minutes," said Lester's mother. That was 5 minutes under the time it had taken Lester to walk home slowly. Lester reached down and tickled him under the chin. "So far out of ten trials, you knew when I was coming home nine times." He got down on his hands and knees and nuzzled his face into Bill Gates's neck. Then he tossed himself into the hammock his father had strung between two trees. He rolled around in it, feeling like he was in a cocoon. Then he imagined himself shedding his skin and blossoming into a beautiful butterfly.

Meanwhile, Bart was waiting on the steps when George arrived home.

"He's been sitting here for the past fifteen minutes," said George's mother. That's how long it had taken George to walk from Vivien's dance school home.

"Can't fool you, can I?" said George. He gave Bart a treat, then went up to his room to fill in his logbook.

Dear Dr. Sheldrake,

Do you think there is plant and animal life on other planets? Do you think the planets can affect our life here? Sometimes when I look at the sky I get the feeling that it's looking back. Did that ever happen to you?

Yours,

George Masson

P.S. Do you know what a mantra is? And did you ever have one? Do you think they work?

Dear George,

I don't think there are animals or plants on any other planet in our solar system. Either the planets are too hot for life as we know it, or too inhospitable in other ways.

Space probes have been sent to the Moon, Mars, and past some of the other planets, and although it's plausible, so far there's no direct evidence of anything living there.

Still, every star you see in the sky is a sun like ours, and hundreds of planets have been found moving round them. Because they are so far away, we don't know if these other planets are like Earth, with animals and plants and other forms of life. But because the universe is huge, with billions of galaxies made up of billions of stars, it seems very likely that some of them could have biological life on them, although it may be very different from what we see on Earth. The fact is no one knows. It's like a blank sheet on which people can project their imaginations. That could be why so much science fiction is about space travel, ETs, and invaders from outer space.

I used to live in India, where I did research in agriculture, and in India lots of people have mantras. They don't necessarily have to mean anything. I have tried chanting a mantra and found that by repeating it as I breathed I was able to focus my mind. I also felt very different and much more connected, with a sense of wholeness.

Best wishes,
Rupert Sheldrake

22

On Tuesday during recess George grabbed a basketball and began to shoot a few baskets. He dribbled over to Lester. "Catch," he said.

"I'm no good," said Lester, dropping the ball.

"It doesn't matter," said George. "You can get good." George threw the ball to Lester, who tried to dribble but kept losing the ball. "Things change. You said so yourself. Remember, I used to hate mustard. You'll get the hang of it," said George. "You just have to practice."

Lester shrugged. "Okay," he said. "I'll take a shot at it."

Lester stood on the foul line and tossed the ball into the air. It bumped the rim and fell to the ground. Lester tried a second time, then a third. On his fourth attempt, the ball rolled around the rim and dropped into the basket.

"See?" said George.

Lester smiled. Another virtue had been released—Persistence—and he'd scored.

When the bell rang to return to class, Ms. Clover asked the students for a progress report on their science experiments.

"I don't want to know details," she said. "But I'd like to know if you've made any discoveries, expected or unexpected."

Charlotte was the first to raise her hand. She had discovered that hamsters don't like to be woken up. "They get grumpy," she said. "Then they bite."

Marcia spoke next. She was trying to discover whether ants preferred sugar or cheese. "If you leave cheese out it starts to stink. And don't put the sugar where your little brother can get it."

"You shouldn't put anything where your little brother can get it," said Charlotte. The class laughed, then Ms. Clover called on Lester.

"I discovered that my dog, Bill Gates, knows when I'm coming home," said Lester. "I kind of knew that already, though. But I discovered some other things too that don't really have to do with the experiment."

"Such as?" said Ms. Clover.

Lester paused while the class looked on. "There are some things about Cape Cod that I really like," he said. "Like the marsh, George, and his dog, Bart. And his sister, Vivien. I didn't like it at first, maybe because it was so unfamiliar. And I missed Denver and my life there. Denver is really nice. And I think of it as my home. But maybe I can have two homes, like the birds that go south in the winter."

Ms. Clover turned to speak to the class. "This is one of the things we should all keep in mind," she said. "Sometimes when we do experiments we discover things we aren't even looking for, and that's why it's good to keep an open mind. This doesn't apply just to science experiments by the way, but to life in general."

Ms. Clover wandered over to George's desk. "What about you, George?" she asked.

"Well, I discovered that each time I think I know the answer to a question, another one comes up," said George.

Ms. Clover smiled and spoke to the class again. "I'm afraid that's another thing that applies not only to science but to life as well. And I don't think we'll ever find all the answers."

Ms. Clover looked back at George. "Anything else?" she asked.

"I discovered that you can keep people in your memory even though they've gone away. And sometimes it's as though they are really here." George looked across the room at Lester. "And probably that's true of places too," he said. George fidgeted in his seat. "Oh, and I discovered I like mustard," he added.

The class laughed.

"Thank you, George," said Ms. Clover.

Lester had invited George to come over to his house after school. When they got to the bike rack, Lester checked his watch. It was 3:08. "Did I tell you I have a parrot?" he said.

"I'd love to have a parrot," said George. He hopped onto his bike and followed Lester. "But my mom says there are already too many people talking in the house. I think she's right."

Lester laughed.

Bill Gates was waiting on the walkway when Lester and George arrived. And Lester's mother was sitting on a mat, cross-legged, eyes closed, in the middle of the Sunshine Studio.

"Is that you, Lester?" she said. She opened her eyes just long enough to check the time. "Bill Gates has been waiting for 27 minutes."

"Thanks, Mom," said Lester. "Bill Gates knew when I was coming, but I wonder if he knew George would be with me. Mom, this is George."

"Hello, George," said Lester's mother. She hadn't moved from her spot on the floor. "Nice to meet you."

"How does she know it's nice to meet me?" whispered George. "Her eyes are closed."

"I'm sure she can feel you," said Lester.

George was puzzled. "What's she doing, anyway?" he asked.

"She's meditating," said Lester. "She's getting calm, centered, and peaceful. She's living in the present."

"Oh," said George. He didn't really get it. "What does that do?"

Lester shrugged. "It's supposed to make you feel good," he said. "I guess it must work because she always feels good."

George nodded, taking in the quiet that surrounded him. It almost seemed to have a sound.

"My house is never this quiet," he said. "I don't think it's possible with a little sister."

A voice from the kitchen broke the silence. "What's up, big guy?"

"That's Carlos," said Lester, leading George into the kitchen.

"Hi there," said George, reaching a finger out to pet the parrot. "What else can you say?"

"He knows about fifty words, but most of the time he says the same thing," said Lester, reaching his hand into a cookie jar filled with crackers. He took one and offered it to Carlos. "Want one?" he said to George.

"Sure," said George. "Thanks."

Lester handed one to George, then took one for himself.

"Just one, Lester dear," chirped Carlos. "Just one, Lester dear."

"Okay, okay," said Lester, turning to George. "Carlos has me on a diet."

Dear Dr. Sheldrake,

Do you think birds are smart? I was thinking how every year spring comes at a different time but the birds always know when the last frost is finished. And they know from far away. Why do you think that is? Also, when they call on the salt marsh, I could swear they are talking to one another, saying something meaningful, even though I can't understand it.

And when they fly they swoop all together. I wonder how they keep their pattern.

Sometimes I wish I were a bird. Did you ever wish to be a bird or some other animal?

Sincerely,

George Masson

P.S. My friend Lester has a parrot that knows fifty words. I think that's a lot for a parrot.

Dear George,

I think some birds are very smart and some are definitely smarter than others. Some of the smartest ones are members of the parrot and crow families. In laboratory experiments crows, magpies, ravens, and jays do really smart things. For example, people test their intelligence by hiding objects and seeing if the bird can find them. Sometimes if one bird watches another one hiding food, it will go and steal it when the first bird has gone away. Other times before hiding something birds will look around to make sure there are no other birds watching so that it won't get stolen.

The smartest bird I've ever come across is an African gray parrot called N'Kisi. He lives in New York State and has a huge vocabulary, about 1,500 words, which is a world record (even fifty is quite a lot for a parrot). He uses language meaningfully and doesn't just "parrot" or mime things. Most surprising, he seems to pick up the thoughts of his owner, Aimee. We've done an experiment in which Aimee sat in one room and opened an envelope containing a picture that someone else had selected. The photos were of things that N'Kisi knew the words for, like "flower" or "car." We filmed N'Kisi in another room while Aimee was looking at the pictures. There was no one with the parrot and he couldn't see Aimee. But in many of the tests he said what Aimee was looking at. He seemed to be picking up her thoughts.

No one really understands how birds know when to migrate or how they find their way over thousands of miles. Some scientists think their ability to find their way may have to do with magnetism, but that's not enough to explain how they get the timing right, or even how they find the right place.

I've always wondered what it would be like to fly, and when I was your age, I sometimes had dreams in which I flew. I don't have them much now, which is a shame because I really enjoyed them.

Yours,

Rupert Sheldrake

23

On Wednesday, Charlotte brought her two hamsters to school. Normally, hamsters sleep during the day and are awake at night. Charlotte was investigating at home how their behavior changed if one of them was roused during the day when it would normally be sleeping. She wanted to find out if the rested hamster remained more alert than the one she'd roused.

"That's Adam," said Charlotte, pointing to the one curled up on a bed of paper shavings in a corner of the cage. "And this is Eve." Eve was spinning a wheel with her tiny feet. Charlotte opened the cage and lifted Eve, cupping the hamster in her hands. Then she walked slowly along the arc of desks so that everyone could meet the hamster. When she got to Lester he petted Eve on the head.

"Hi," he said.

"Want to hold her?" asked Charlotte.

"Sure," said Lester, gently taking the hamster. Eve sniffed wildly, then settled into Lester's hand.

"She likes you," said Charlotte. She seemed happy about this.

"Why do you think that might be?" Ms. Clover asked the class.

"It might be his smell," said someone.

"Or the temperature of his hands," said someone else.

"Maybe it's because he's nice," said Charlotte.

"It could be any or all of those," said Ms. Clover. "But how could we test some of those variables?"

"Give Lester a perfumed bubble bath and change his diet," said George.

The class laughed.

"That's right," said Ms. Clover. "We would have to control for smell while keeping other variables constant. Then we could control for body temperature."

"Then we'd ask Lester to be mean," said someone.

"I'm not sure Lester could be mean," said Ms. Clover.

Lester let out a low growl, startling the hamster. Then Charlotte lifted Eve from Lester's hands and continued along the arc of desks.

"I think Charlotte likes you," George said to Lester as they walked toward the bike rack after school.

"You do?" said Lester.

"She thinks you're nice," said George. "That means she likes you."

"Maybe I should invite her to my birthday party," said Lester. His birthday was a few weeks off.

"Why not?" said George. He and Lester hopped onto their bikes and sped off together, parting ways at Plum and Prune streets.

When Lester got home, Bill Gates had been waiting for 15 minutes.

"Atta boy," said Lester, ruffling Bill Gates's fur. Bill Gates followed Lester up to his room and Lester filled in his logbook. Then he opened his notebook and doodled a birthday cake.

"I'm going to start making a list of whom I'm inviting to my birthday," he said to Bill Gates. "Of course you can come. And George, and Vivien." Then he added Charlotte's name. Beside it he did a quick doodle of Adam and Eve.

Meanwhile, when George arrived home, Bart was waiting on the porch steps.

"Thirteen minutes," said Mrs. Masson, who was putting the finishing touches on a birthday cake.

"Lester's birthday is coming up," said George. "We can make him a cake."

"Or a pie," said Vivien, who was licking a beater. "He loves pies."

"I've never heard of a birthday pie," said George.

"We can invent one," said Vivien.

George went to his room and filled in his logbook. Then he opened the drawer where he kept his T-shirts. Beneath the neat piles was the boomerang that Kyra had given him before leaving. George had tried throwing it, but he'd never gotten it to come back.

George slipped the boomerang into his belt. "Come on, Bart," he said, heading for the yard. He flung the boomerang into the air, and when it didn't return, Bart fetched it and dropped it at George's feet. George threw it again and again, with Bart retrieving it each time, until finally it seemed to pause in midair, fall backward, then spin around, landing at his feet.

"Hey," cried George. "I did it."

That evening Kyra texted him. "We're coming the beginning of July for a visit."

24

On Thursday something unexpected happened. Ms. Clover let George and Lester out of school fifteen minutes before the bell rang so they could see if their dogs knew they were coming home early.

Both boys hopped on their bikes and sped home as fast as they could.

Lester pulled into the driveway and started up the walkway. Bill Gates was waiting at the gate.

"What are you doing home so early?" said Lester's mother. "Are you feeling all right?"

"I feel great," said Lester. "Ms. Clover let us out early." Lester nuzzled Bill Gates's fur, "And you knew, didn't you?" he said.

"He's been there 5 minutes," said Lester's mother. It had taken Lester 10 minutes to bike home.

Lester filled in his logbook. Then he went into the yard and picked up a ball. "Fetch," he cried, tossing it to Bill Gates.

Just then a yelp came from the neighboring yard. "What was that?" said Lester. He peeked between the hedges and there was Mrs. Robarts racing out of the toolshed. And Mr. Robarts was following. They disappeared into the house.

Lester stayed glued to the hedges until things quieted down.

When George got home at 2:56, Bart was on the steps waiting.

"What are you doing here?" said Zac, who was parking his bike in the garage. "Did you get kicked out of school?"

"I got out early to test Bart," said George. "It's part of my experiment."

"I'd like an experiment like that," said Zac.

"Bart's been waiting 7 minutes," said George's mother, who was loading cakes into her pastry van.

George petted Bart, then went off to fill in his logbook.

When he went back downstairs he found Vivien lying on the floor reading a book aloud. George took out his homework and joined her.

"It's about dogs," said Vivien. "It says dogs are man's best friend—"

George interrupted her. "It should say 'person's' best friend. In the old days 'man' meant everyone."

"What does it mean in the new days?" asked Vivien.

"It means grownup guy."

"Oh," said Vivien. "Like you."

"Sort of," said George, smiling to himself.

"I think it should say boy's best friend," said Vivien, laughing.

25

On Friday Vivien was supposed to meet George outside the entrance of school. But she wasn't there. George looked around for Madeleine.

"Have you seen Vivien?" he asked.

"She went that way," said Madeleine. "She was following Lester."

George started off in the direction of Lester's house. As he neared the hedges, he could see Vivien's bright yellow sneakers poking out from beneath the foliage.

"Vivien," cried George. She turned around.

"What are you doing here?" said George. "You were supposed to meet me."

Vivien crawled out from beneath the hedges. "Lester dropped his hat and I wanted to give it back to him," she said.

"So why haven't you?" said George.

"I did," said Vivien.

"Then what are you still doing here?" asked George. He crouched down and looked through the hedges. "You're spying on Lester."

Vivien shook her head. "No," she said. "I'm spying on his neighbor. The criminal lady."

"We don't know if she's a criminal," said George.

"I've never met a criminal," said Vivien.

"I don't think you're missing anything," said George, tugging on Vivien's ankles.

"I think she eats dog biscuits," said Vivien.

"Why do you think that?" asked George.

"I saw her in the garden with some on her tea plate," said Vivien.

"Are you sure?" asked George, trying not to smile.

"Yes, I'm sure," said Vivien. "And she looked guilty."

"How do you mean, 'guilty'?" asked George.

"Like this," said Vivien, raising her eyebrows and screwing her mouth into a tiny O.

George took Vivien by the arm. "Come on," he said.

When they got home, Bart wasn't at the top of the stairs. He was asleep on the floor at the foot of George's bed. It was only the second time in nearly three weeks that he hadn't been waiting.

George's mother was planting pansies in the garden. "Bart's been restless all day. I think he knew there was work to be done. I could have used him to dig some holes, but he's decided to nap."

"I'll help dig," said Vivien. She loved to get down in the dirt.

"Change your clothes first," said Mrs. Masson.

George went up to his room. "Hey, big guy," he said to Bart. "You feeling okay?"

Vivien poked her head through the doorway. She'd put on her overalls and pulled her hair back into a ponytail.

"Don't worry," she said to George. "It's just an experiment. That's what you said. Besides Bart knows when you're coming most of the time."

George sat down to record the day's results in his logbook. Vivien tiptoed toward him and peeked over his shoulder.

"Do you think scientists ever cheat?" she said.

"Why are you asking?" said George.

Vivien shrugged. "I don't know," she said. "It just seems like it would be easy."

"I don't know," said George.

"But what do you think?" asked Vivien.

George shrugged. Vivien had asked what he thought. And he couldn't answer. How could that be? He was thinking all the time.

"Probably not on purpose," said George at last. But he wasn't really sure. If wanting the results to come out a certain way was cheating, then maybe they did cheat. Maybe he was cheating. Maybe it couldn't be helped. It was part of being human.

"Do you want me to plant you a pansy, George?" asked Vivien.

"Sure," said George.

"I'm going to plant one for Dad and Zac and Bart," Vivien continued. "And Lester, and Bill Gates."

"Good," said George. "Then there'll be a lot of flowers." The thought made him happy.

Dear Dr. Sheldrake,

Do scientists ever cheat when they do experiments? Do you think wanting an experiment to turn out in a certain way is cheating? I guess it would be hard to know if a scientist was cheating or not.

Yours truly,

George Masson

Dear George,

Scientists are people like everybody else. Some people cheat in school or in business and some don't. Some politicians tell lies and others are honest. Scientists are like that too. Some of them cheat and sometimes they're found out. Years ago there was a case of a brilliant young scientist who kept making impressive discoveries. He published articles in important scientific journals, and even won three prestigious awards. But other people couldn't seem to get his experiments to work for them. As it turned out, he'd been making up a lot of his results. When he was found out, he lost his job and the papers he had published were all retracted by the journals, which means they told people not to believe them anymore.

I don't think wanting something to happen is cheating. If I want to win a game, it's not cheating. In fact, if I played Monopoly or baseball and I didn't want to win, I probably wouldn't. So wanting something to happen isn't cheating. It gives you a motive for doing it. But making up results is cheating and that's wrong in science, as it is in ordinary life. With your experiments with Bart, what you find out is only interesting if people can believe what you say. If you were making it up, that wouldn't be science. In fact, it would be anti-science because you would be deceiving people to try to make them believe things that are false. So it's important to be honest in science, like in everything else. And if you are not honest, when people find out they won't trust you or your work anymore.

Best wishes,
Rupert Sheldrake

26

On Saturday morning, Mr. Masson was up with the birds. "Who wants to take the sailboat down to the shore with me?" he asked. Each spring, the Massons anchored the boat to a wooden dock at the end of the marsh, where it stayed until fall.

"I can't," said Vivien. She was staring at three tiny cacti she had planted in a clay pot. "I'm watching the cacti grow."

"You can't see anything," said Zac, who was about to go on a bike ride. "They grow too slowly. Can you watch your hand grow, or your fingers?" Zac didn't wait for Vivien to answer. "No," he told her. "Because it happens too slowly."

George stretched out his hand in front of him. There seemed to be so much happening there, his pulse, the blood flowing. But no, he couldn't see it growing. George had never thought about the things you didn't see because they happened so slowly. But come to think of it, they were all around him. Like his starting to like Lester. It was so slow he'd barely noticed it happening. But it had. Lester had become his friend.

"I'll go," said George, helping to mount the sailboat onto its trolley. Bart barked. He wanted to go too.

They followed the path in back of the house, the one that ripened with spring visitors until it became a well-worn trail. George walked alongside his father, one hand on the trolley. When they got to the shore, they released the boat into the water. It bounced and settled comfortably into its new surroundings. George felt a wave of nostalgia wash over him as they moored it to the dock. Kyra had loved bobbing on the water, pointing out the wildlife.

George and his father started back across the marsh. They crossed a wooden bridge over a stream that flowed into the sea. Beneath them, the alewives had started their journey from the salty currents to spawn in the fresh water. George stopped to watch. He knew that many of the fish would never make it back. Instead, they would end up beached on the sand flats, prey to the gulls and seabirds, who stood watch. He couldn't understand why they threw themselves so willingly into what must be certain death. Maybe it was instinct, like Rupert Sheldrake said, the same thing that made the caterpillars return year after year.

George looked at his father. "Why do you think they do that when there's a good chance they'll die?" he asked.

Mr. Masson was thoughtful. "I suppose it's because they have a faith in the way of things. In the way of life."

George nodded. Maybe instinct was that too, a faith in the way of things. They continued on in silence. For a moment, George thought that he could feel his hand growing. Maybe it wasn't his hand, but all of him. Then he felt his father's hand on the back of his neck.

George thought how he always wanted to know the hows and whys of everything. That's one of the reasons he loved science. But maybe sometimes you couldn't know why. Or maybe the why was changing. George thought about the caterpillars. Maybe they weren't that smart. But maybe they had a faith in the way of things too.

27

On Sunday, Lester and Bill Gates joined George and Bart on the mudflats where the marsh joined into the sea. Lester was growing accustomed to the squishy ground under his feet. Each time he walked there it was like blazing a trail in his mind that made it more familiar and, therefore, more comfortable.

Bill Gates ran ahead in search of Bart, who was poking his nose into the sand, searching for clams and crabs. Bart's ears perked up as Bill Gates approached, and the two dogs circled each other playfully until the cry of a bird sent them frolicking across the cordgrass. The marsh was teeming with new life—hummingbirds and bees, eider ducks, ospreys, crabs, and freshwater clams. Less than a month ago, it had been barren.

George put his fingers to his lips and whistled. A bird whistled back. "Hey, why do you think they call people birdbrains?" George asked. "That means you're dumb, but birds aren't dumb." He thought how the birds abandoned the marsh at the first sign of a freeze and returned with the spring thaw, how the swallows dipped and dived in unison as though they were one, how Alabaster the pigeon knew to return to the loft. "Birdbrain" was a compliment as far as George could tell.

"I don't know," said Lester. He'd wrapped Bill Gates's leash around his ankles and was spiraling like a top to unwind it. Then Lester kicked off his sneakers, rolled up his pant legs, and took a running jump that ended with him knee deep in water. "Ah," he cried. "It's cold."

Bill Gates bounded back across the marsh and looked at Lester as if to say, "Why did you do a silly thing like that?"

"I just couldn't help myself," said Lester. "I felt this strange and mysterious push."

George was reminded of the fortune-teller and how he'd felt compelled to consult her. Maybe that was instinct too. He waited to see if he might feel the same push. But he didn't. Still, he kicked off his sneakers, rolled up his pant legs, and walked boldly into the ice-cold water, clutching his teeth to keep from crying out. There was a moment of towering silence. Then a tern appeared, the first of the season, galloping across the sand flats flaunting its black-and-white forked tail. Bart and Bill Gates looked at each other knowingly and were off in eager pursuit. But before they could get there the tern had taken flight and was soaring high above their heads.

"I used to be afraid to put my head underwater," George confessed. Then he corrected himself. "I don't know if I was really afraid, but I didn't like it."

"There's nothing to be afraid of," said Lester. "Just pretend that you're a fish."

"That's exactly what Kyra told me to do," said George.

"Who's Kyra?" asked Lester.

"A friend of mine," said George. "She used to live here, but she moved to North Carolina."

"Does she like it there?" asked Lester.

"She says it's different, but yeah," said George. "Kyra finds something to like about everything."

"I guess that's a virtue," said Lester.

"I guess so," said George.

Lester waded out of the water. "When I don't like something, my dad always says, 'Lester, dear, in life you have to move forward. Don't look back.'"

George smiled. He thought it was funny that Lester's father called him dear.

Lester plucked a thick strand of grass and pressed it between his two thumbs. Then he whistled, causing a general flutter across the marsh.

"Do you think you can have a girl friend who's not a girlfriend?" George asked.

"Sure," said Lester. "But I don't think you can have a girlfriend who's not a girl friend."

"Did you ever have a girlfriend?" George asked.

"I really liked this girl in Denver," said Lester. "I got butterflies in my stomach when I thought about her. I'd start to sweat. I even lost my appetite, which hardly ever happens. But I guess she didn't feel the same."

None of those things happened when George looked at Kyra. He just felt a nice warm sensation like he was glowing inside.

"I guess love is complicated," said George. "That kind of love, anyway."

Suddenly Lester spread his arms wide and began flapping like a bird, releasing all the energy that was pent up inside him, letting go as he swooped and soared. Then George spread his arms wide and followed. The birds and the dogs stopped to stare, and for one brief moment George was sure the world had stopped.

"I wonder what it feels like to be a bird," said Lester. "Or a strand of cordgrass."

"Or a cloud," said George, throwing back his head and looking upward.

It started to rain and George stuck out his tongue to catch the drops, which were the size of bullets. Lester caught some too.

"You know, even the rain tastes different here than in Denver," he said.

"Yes," said George. "But, Lester, dear, in life we must move forward."

George and Bart dropped Lester and Bill Gates at home, then took a detour, passing by the house where Kyra used to live. George stopped, and Bart waited patiently as he looked at the gray weathered cape, similar to Lester's house. An immense quiet seemed to flow back to him. The driveway was empty and the garage door was down. The Joyners had had three little windmills on the roof to measure the velocity and direction of the wind, but they were no longer there. George felt a wave of sadness wash through his body. He tried to stay with it and locate just where it was, but it seemed to move from one part to another. Without even thinking, he reached down and touched the green ribbon on his wrist. Then he took a deep breath, and it was like a cool breeze circling him, carrying the remnants of Kyra— Kyra particles, George called them—away. George's gaze settled on an abandoned lawn chair in the yard, and for the first time he realized fully that Kyra was gone. Then a hush settled over the house, a long, drawn-out "Ssh."

"How could a house say 'Ssh'?" George whispered. Then he turned to Bart. "Come on, big guy," he said. "Let's go home."

28

Lester woke up on Monday with a queasy stomach and no appetite. That was unusual for Lester. He hoped he wasn't getting the flu. He ate a light breakfast of toast and jam—light for Lester, anyway. Then he started for school on foot. He was looking forward to geography class. Ms. Clover was showing a movie about Africa, which she'd visited last summer.

Lester entered the schoolyard and walked past the bike rack. He looked to the right, expecting to see George's bike. But the slot was empty. George must have walked or gotten a ride.

Ms. Clover took attendance, but when she called George's name, there was no answer. George was absent. Lester wondered if he wasn't feeling well either.

After school, Lester took the long way home, walking past George's house. The car wasn't in the driveway and the pastry van was gone. When Lester arrived home, he found Bill Gates in the kitchen.

"He's been there over an hour," said Lester's mother.

Lester stroked Bill Gates's back. "Is something wrong, buddy?" he said. Lester checked his watch—3:40—and went upstairs to fill in his logbook. When he was done, he came back down to the kitchen. "Come on," he said to Bill Gates. "Let's go to the marsh."

Lester tossed a tennis ball and Bill Gates raced off to fetch it, through the strands of cordgrass, across the wooden bridge. Lester had hoped that George might show up. But he didn't.

Bill Gates raced back with the tennis ball in his mouth. He dropped it at Lester's feet, then rubbed up against his leg.

"What are you thinking?" said Lester. He and Bill Gates headed home, passing George's house for the second time that day. The car was back in the driveway, and the van was parked on the side of the road. Lester thought about ringing the bell but something held him back. He stopped for a minute, seconds in which time seemed to stand still. Then he and Bill Gates kept on walking.

29

George was back at school the next day looking as though he hadn't slept a wink. His clothes were disheveled and his hair uncombed.

"Hey, what's wrong?" asked Lester. "You look more like me than you."

"What's right?" groaned George. "Bart got hit by a car yesterday morning."

In the seconds that followed, something strange happened to Lester. It was like he became George or George became him. He could feel George's pain as though it were his own. It felt awful.

George started to cry tiny tears that spurted from the corners of his eyes. They reminded Lester of mustard squirting from a tube. George tried to quell them with his shirtsleeve.

"Is he going to be okay?" asked Lester

George shook his head. "They don't know yet," he said. "The vet might have to put him to sleep."

Lester reached in his pocket for a napkin. "Here," he said.

"Thanks," said George, wiping his eyes again.

George braved the day silently. During recess, Lester tried to distract him with a basketball, but it was no use. George wouldn't budge from the bench where he sat.

"I'm sure Bart will be all right," said Lester.

"How can you be sure?" asked George. "I'm not sure. So please don't say that."

It was one of those times in life when there wasn't anything more to say, no words to express emotion. So Lester just sat down next to George and said nothing.

Lester stopped at his locker after school, then went to look for George, but George wasn't at his locker or on the playground.

"Anyone seen George?" he asked.

Charlotte answered. "His dad picked him and Vivien up," she said.

Lester walked home alone, thoughts turning in his head like a cyclone.

"Bill Gates has been coming out to the gate on and off all day," said Lester's mother. But he wasn't there now. He was in the backyard.

Lester nodded absently. He looked at his watch. It was 3:41.

"What's wrong?" asked Lester's mother. She put her hand to Lester's forehead. "You look sick."

"I don't feel that well," said Lester. He wondered if bad news could give you a fever. "I think it's because something awful happened. George's dog, Bart, got hit by a car yesterday."

Lester's mother's mouth contracted into a thin hyphen. Then she whispered, "No."

"Yes," said Lester. "And the vet doesn't know if he's going to be okay."

"Poor Bart," said Lester's mother. "And poor George."

Lester's eyes had begun to water. He bent down and rubbed Bill Gates's fur coat. "Now don't you go out and get hit by a car. Please." Tears welled in Lester's eyes at the very thought. "I hope nothing ever happens to you," he said.

Vivien sat on George's bed with her hands in her lap. She'd put on her blue dress with the tiny yellow flowers and fluted sleeves. "It's my lucky dress," she said. "I'm wearing it for Bart." Bart was still at the vet's.

"I'm sure Bart appreciates your wearing it for him," said George. "But I doubt it's going to help." Vivien shrugged.

George looked at his logbook. Bart had been waiting for him 13 out of 15 times. He didn't count Monday when Bart got hit or today when he was at the vet. There were three trials left. But Bart probably wouldn't be able to finish the experiment.

George closed his logbook and stared into space. Now he was the one waiting for Bart to come home. But he wasn't sure that was going to happen.

30

George came to school on Wednesday wearing black from head to toe. "They put Bart to sleep last night," he said to Lester, who was dribbling a basketball on the playground.

Lester stopped what he was doing. "No," he said.

"Yes," said George. He took the basketball and squeezed it between his hands. "Life is weird," he said quietly. "I wonder what it's like to die. It must be strange."

"I don't know," said Lester. "But I think about that sometimes too."

"I wonder if Bart knew he was going to die," said George. "I bet he did. I read somewhere that some people know when they're going to die. They get a feeling. I think Bart had that feeling."

Goose bumps broke out on the surface of Lester's skin. He didn't have that feeling but he had others, like how mysterious life was. An image rose in his mind of the marsh the first time he saw it.

George started to cry again. "I miss Bart," he said, putting his fist to his eyes. "He was like a brother. No, he was better than a brother."

"I miss him too," said Lester, reaching up and grabbing a whirlybird from an overhanging branch. He opened it and stuck it on his nose. Then he handed one to George and George did the same thing. And they stood there in silence until the school bell rang.

George passed the day in a haze, doing his schoolwork like a robot. Nothing felt very real. At recess Ms. Clover came over to him and gave him a hug. "I'm sorry about Bart, George," she said.

George nodded. He could see why she had the word "love" in her name.

George waited for Vivien after school and they started home together. Vivien reached out and took George's hand. George hoped no one was looking. The truth was that Vivien's soft, warm, little hand felt good in his.

"My lucky dress didn't work," said Vivien. "Bart died. That's not lucky at all. But I'm going to wear it for another day just in case."

"I don't think a dress will bring Bart back," said George.

Vivien sighed. "But maybe something else will happen."

"Like what?" asked George.

Vivien shrugged. She let go of George's hand and hugged her book bag to her chest. They crossed over the bridge with the alewives and George recalled what his father had said about their faith in the way of things. He wished he could have that kind of faith.

George hated to go home. He half expected Bart to be there waiting for him, but he knew that was wishful thinking. Instead, his mother greeted him at the door.

George looked at her and she looked back with a strange, motherly knowing, as though she could look right through him. She certainly knew what he was feeling. Maybe it wasn't motherly, George thought, but humanly instead.

After dinner, Vivien went out to the porch to fill the bird feeders hanging from the rafters. She went through the ritual each day, feeling wholly and solemnly responsible for the birds' existence. George understood her desire to keep life going. But he didn't have the heart to tell her it was otherwise, that it depended on other things far bigger than she. Bart proved that.

George went up to his room and sat on his bed. He was wondering how to break the news to Kyra. She'd loved Bart like he had.

There was a knock on George's door. It was his father. "Can I come in?" he said.

"Sure," said George. "So I guess I won't be finishing my experiment."

"I know, George," said his father. He set his hand on

the top of George's head and planted a kiss there. "But isn't this life?"

It sounded to George more like a question than a statement.

"It shouldn't be," mumbled George.

"But I'm afraid it is," said his father.

After Mr. Masson had left the room, George lay down on his bed and texted Kyra. "Something happened. And it's not good," he wrote. "Bart got hit by a car and they put him to sleep. I guess that's life," he added.

It took a while for Kyra to text back. But she did. "It is life, but luckily, life is more than that (smile). I know you are sad and I am sad too. Tonight let's not think of fruit. Instead let's think about all the happy times we had with Bart."

George texted back: "Good idea."

Later, Zac came in. "Hey, big guy," he said. Ordinarily he would have given George a high five, but this time he gave him a hug—a big-brotherly hug. "I got a surprise for you." He led George to the window. George's bike was parked in the driveway below. Zac had painted the spokes in all the colors of the rainbow.

"Wow," said George.

"I'm sorry about Bart," said Zac. "I know he was like a brother to you—sometimes more than me."

"Thanks," said George, realizing how lucky he was

to have a big brother. Suddenly, he was seeing Zac from another angle. It reminded him of when he saw Lester in a different way. Maybe that was life too.

Dear Dr. Sheldrake,

I am writing to tell you that I won't be able to finish my experiment, Dogs Who Know When Their Owners Are Coming Home. That's because my dog, Bart, got hit by a car and had to be put to sleep. I would still like to send you my results if you are interested. I don't know why that had to happen to Bart. And I don't think any experiment will help me to find out. My dad says, "That's life, isn't it?" I guess he's right.

Best regards,
George Masson

P.S. Did you ever have a pet that died?

Dear George,

I'm very sorry to hear about Bart's death. It must be really upsetting, especially since you had so little warning. I have had a lot of pets over the years and of course have seen many of them die. I was very sad when our cat died a few years ago. We buried him in the garden and there's a rosebush growing over him now.

Yes, I'd love to see the results of your experiment with

Bart. Obviously, you couldn't finish the planned number of trials because of his death, but the others will still be very helpful data, so please send them to me.

Best wishes,

Rupert Sheldrake

31

Friday, George presented the results of his experiment to the class, four weeks after it had begun.

"For my science project I participated in an experiment designed by Rupert Sheldrake called 'Dogs Who Know When Their Owners Are Coming Home,'" he said.

"Dr. Sheldrake is a scientist who studies plant and animal behavior," he explained. "He noticed that there were many people who felt that their dogs knew when they were coming home. And he decided to try to prove this. He gathered information from more than two thousand pet owners and discovered that in many of these cases a dog's anticipation of its owner's arrival could not be explained by routine, clues from people at home, the sound of a familiar car approaching, or by anything else we know about in science."

George continued. "Sheldrake observed that most people whose dogs could anticipate their arrival were very attached to their dog. So he wondered if the dogs were reacting to their owners' thoughts, feelings, emotions, or intentions."

George held up his logbook. He'd pasted a photo of Bart on the cover.

"This is me and my dog, Bart," he said. "Bart always seemed to know when I was coming home. So I decided to test it out. I varied my schedule and arrival time from school every day for fifteen days. I arrived home anytime between 2:56 and 5:30. And I recorded the exact time that I started for home from wherever I was. I didn't include weekends because I wasn't sure there'd be someone at home to record the results. I kept a logbook of the days and times when Bart went to the step. And I tried not to have any expectations of what might happen, because some scientists say that even what you think can affect the outcome." George's voice faltered, but he went on. "And then just last Monday Bart got hit by a car and died."

George shifted his weight from one leg to the other. "I guess that's why you need a lot of people doing the same experiment, different people with different ideas," he added. "Because it's impossible to control or even to know all the things that might affect an experiment. Like maybe your dog dying."

George looked at his classmates. A wave of compassion swept through the room.

"Another thing happened too," said George. "When I started the experiment, I decided to write to Rupert Sheldrake and ask him some of the questions I had. I didn't think he'd write back to me, but he did. And I learned lots about not only dog behavior but animal behavior in general. And I learned some things about people behavior too. Like if you write to really important people, they might write back." George stopped. "I also learned that even though you're younger, you can win a bet with your older brother. And I learned that I should have faith in things. But that's hard."

The class let out a group sigh, and George managed a smile.

"Anyway," said George. "Bart didn't get to finish the twenty trials. But he knew when I was coming home in thirteen out of fifteen, which is 86.6 percent of the time. It didn't matter at what time I arrived, if I came by car, on my bike, or if I walked. Bart would be waiting on the second step of the front porch, and he'd gone out there within minutes of when I'd started to think about going home. There were only two times when he wasn't waiting for me. The first time he was chasing a mole in the garden and I think he was distracted. I know sometimes when I get distracted I forget things. The second time Bart wasn't waiting was the Friday before he got hit by the car. My sister, Vivien, was supposed to wait for me after school. But she wasn't there. So my thoughts about going home were interrupted by thoughts of finding my sister. Also, my mother noticed that Bart had been restless all day, so it could be that he had some premonition that something was going to happen to him. But I guess we'll never know.

"In conclusion," said George, "my results support Rupert Sheldrake's theory that there is an invisible connection between some dogs and their owners, which allows them to communicate in ways we don't yet understand."

George thanked the class and took his seat. Then Lester stood up and walked to the front of the classroom to present his results. He'd forgotten to comb his hair and there was a thin trail of hot chocolate etched across his T-shirt. But that didn't seem to bother him.

"I got my dog, Bill Gates, when I was four," said Lester, holding up a picture of his dog. "And from early on it was clear to me and my parents that he knew when I was about to come home. It didn't matter where I came from—school, the golf course, the dentist—Bill Gates would be in the driveway waiting for me."

Lester stopped to take a deep breath, then went on. "When we moved here, it was the same, maybe even more so. I think that was because Bill Gates didn't have any friends. It could be that he was lonely. But then he made friends with Bart, George's dog."

Lester stopped to rub his eyes. "Bill Gates took part

in the experiment for sixteen days," he said. "And he was waiting when I got home thirteen of those days. So that's 81.25 percent and that's significant. We were supposed to continue the experiment for another week, but we stopped when Bart got hit by the car because I felt that might have influenced the results. There were only three days in which Bill Gates wasn't waiting. The first time was the first day of the experiment. And I think it might have been because when I thought about going home, I was thinking about Denver and not Cape Cod. And I think that might have confused Bill Gates. The second time was the day that George's dog, Bart, got hit by a car. Bill Gates was in the kitchen when I got home. The third time was the day after. Bill Gates went out to the walkway several times during the day, but when I got home he was in the backyard. I think that's because he knew something had happened. Maybe I knew too, because the morning that Bart got hit by a car I felt queasy and lost my appetite and that never happens to me."

The class giggled uncomfortably.

"So I think all this means that I'm connected to Bart and George in some unknown way. Maybe part of me knew what was happening. And maybe Bart was connected to Bill Gates."

Lester sat down in his seat.

"Thank you, Lester," said Ms. Clover. She turned to the class. "I think what Lester is trying to say is that although he set out to prove that he and his dog were connected, he discovered that maybe this phenomenon isn't specific to pets and people. Maybe all of life is connected by some form of knowing we can't yet explain."

There was a big hush in the classroom.

George raised his hand.

"George," said Ms. Clover. "Is there something you would like to add?"

George stood up. "I'm proud of Bart for having done his part for science," he said. "And even though he's dead I think Bart is still connected to me. And I hope when I die and go to heaven Bart will know that I'm coming and be waiting for me."

Ms. Clover cleared her throat. Her eyes had begun to water. George wondered if she might even cry.

"Thank you, George, for sharing that with the class," she said. "And thank you, Lester."

After school, George walked Vivien home.

"What do you think is up there?" Vivien asked, looking skyward.

"Clouds," said George. "Gases. Stars. Planets. The sun. Probably there are other universes out there with other forms of life."

"Do you think there's anything else?" she asked.

"Like what?" asked George.

"I don't know," said Vivien. "Maybe a butterfly jungle. Or a dog city. Something like that."

"Could be," said George.

"I think there must be," said Vivien.

George hoped so.

Dear Dr. Sheldrake,

My dog, Bart, knew that I was coming home 13 out of 15 times. My friend Lester did the experiment, and his dog, Bill Gates, knew when he was coming 13 out of 16 times.

But something strange happened. The Friday before Bart got hit by a car, he didn't come out to meet me. And the day that Bart got hit, Bill Gates wasn't waiting for Lester. Also Lester felt sick to his stomach, which never happens. Then the day that Bart died, Bill Gates went out to wait for Lester a few times. But when Lester got home he was in the backyard. So I am wondering if maybe Bart, Bill Gates, and Lester somehow had a feeling that something was going to happen. Do you think this is possible? Maybe we are connected too.

Sincerely,

George Masson

Dear George,

Of course, it's hard to know what was going on with these reactions before Bart's death. Some animals do seem able to pick up on what's about to happen, particularly if it's something frightening or dangerous. Many animals behave with signs of fear or anxiety before earthquakes or tsunamis. Sometimes this happens several days in advance. No one knows how they do it, but in China they've used it as an effective way of predicting earthquakes and have saved hundreds of thousands of lives. Some animals also seem to know when their owners are going to have accidents and show signs of fear or behave in other unusual ways. Again no one understands how this happens, but it does seem to. It happens to people too. So maybe Bart and Lester were both picking up on something that was going to happen. But this is not the kind of thing we can do research on through experiments, and it's something we can never be sure about.

Thank you for sending along your results, which I will add to my data files.

Best wishes,
Rupert Sheldrake

32

Lester opened a fresh bag of dog biscuits for Bill Gates, then they headed off toward the marsh. George was already there. He was standing on the point of land that reached farthest into the sea, watching a blue heron construct a nest. Lester joined him.

"It's strange," said George. "Bart isn't here, but it's like I can still hear him barking. I know it's just my imagination but it seems so real."

"I know what you mean," said Lester. "Sometimes if I close my eyes it feels like I'm still in Denver. But I'm not. It's weird, isn't it?"

"It's the same with Alabaster," said George. "She was one of the homing pigeons that lived there in a loft in that outbuilding." George pointed into the distance. "She flew away right before Kyra moved, and never came back. No one knew why. Sometimes I think I see her."

George squinted. "Like now," he added. There on the roof of the outbuilding was a pigeon.

"Alabaster," whispered George. He started toward the building, followed by Lester and Bill Gates, unable to believe what he saw until he was looking into the bird's face, eye to eye. This time it wasn't his imagination. It was Alabaster. She'd returned to the marsh.

"Hey, what are you doing here?" said George out loud. Was it the other birds who were returning to the marsh? George wondered. Was it George himself? Or maybe it was Bart.

Alabaster flew over to George and perched on his shoulder just like she used to do.

"This is Lester," said George. "And, Lester, this is Alabaster."

The pigeon's head darted from one boy to the other. Then she hopped over onto Lester's shoulder.

Bill Gates began to bark, but Lester quieted him. "Ssh. Hi, little guy," he said to the pigeon.

"It's a girl," said George.

"Maybe she missed you," said Lester.

"Maybe," said George. But he suspected there was more to it. George didn't think he could ever prove it, but maybe it didn't matter. He'd realized that there was a knowing that was bigger than proof. It was the great and wondrous knowing of nature, of the alewives, of the birds who knew when it was time to return to the marsh each year.

George set the dinner table, listening for the sound of his father's jeep. He couldn't wait to share the news.

"You won't believe what happened," he said at dinner. "Alabaster came back to the marsh today."

Mr. Masson's eyebrows popped up in surprise. "Alabaster the pigeon?" he said.

"Why is that so hard to believe?" said Vivien.

"She's been gone for months," said George.

"Maybe it took her that long to find the way," said Zac.

"Or maybe she came back to see you, George, because she knew that Bart died," said Vivien.

"I think Vivien could be right," said Mrs. Masson.

There was a moment of silence, one of few in the Masson household. Then Vivien spoke.

"I bumped into Lester and Bill Gates on the way to Madeleine's house," she said. "They were walking home from the marsh."

"And so?" said Zac.

"We made an amazing discovery," she said.

All eyes turned to Vivien. "Well?" said George, noticing that she was still wearing her lucky dress.

Vivien cleared her throat. "We found out what Lester's neighbor is hiding in her toolshed." She pursed her lips and her voice fell to a whisper. "And she isn't a criminal, by the way."

"Phew," teased Zac, brushing his forehead. "Well, what is it?" he asked. "The suspense is killing me."

"A dog," said Vivien. "A little puppy." Vivien held her hands out about one foot apart. "She found it, but Mr. Robarts doesn't want it in the house. He doesn't like dogs. So she's been keeping it in the toolshed."

"How'd you find that out?" asked Zac. "Were you spying again?"

"Just a little," said Vivien. "But Mrs. Robarts caught us and asked Lester if he wanted another dog. He said Bill Gates was enough, but he knew of someone who might want one." Vivien turned to George.

"That's a nice idea," said Mr. Masson. "But I don't know if George is ready for another dog just yet."

"Are you, George?" said Viven. "Maybe?"

George was focused on the tiny flowers on Vivien's dress. Could a dress really be lucky? he wondered.

George shrugged. "It might remind me of Bart," he said.

"Don't you want to be reminded of Bart?" asked Vivien.

George wasn't sure. "Maybe," he said.

"So why don't you meet the puppy and see if you like it?" said Vivien.

George thought for a moment. "Okay," he said.

"Oh, and another thing," said Vivien. "I saw Mrs. Robarts eating a dog biscuit. She took a big bite."

"Really?" said Zac, chuckling.

Vivien folded her arms across her chest. "Cross my heart," she said.

Mrs. Masson tried to keep from laughing. "I'm sure she was just curious," she said. "I can see how that might happen."

"I can't," said Zac, shaking his head.

"Me either," said Mr. Masson.

"That's because you don't have any imagination," said Vivien.

George was pensive. He had just noticed something strange, or at least he thought it was strange. Mrs. Robarts had the word "Bart" in her name.

Dear Dr. Sheldrake,

Do you think a pigeon could return to a place it knew because it missed it, or the people there? I've read about dogs who return to their own homes, but I don't know about birds.

Yours truly,
George Masson

P.S. Did you ever wonder how a dog biscuit tasted? Or did you ever try one?

Dear George,

Lots of animals are really attached to their homes and don't like being away, which is why we see homing behavior in pigeons, dogs, cats, and many other species.

Pigeons can definitely return to their homes. In fact, a lot of them are called homing pigeons because they do just that. In America there are hundreds of thousands of people who keep pigeons as a hobby and they race them against each other. The same happens here in Europe. The pigeons are put in a basket and taken away from their home, sometimes as far as 600 miles away. Then they are released at a recorded time. They fly up into the sky and circle a few times and then head off toward their home. Some arrive the very same day, covering 600 miles in about ten hours which is an average speed of about 60 miles per hour. Usually some of their family are left in the loft, and, in fact, they race home more quickly if they have been taken away from mates and young.

Migrating birds find their way over thousands of miles. The arctic tern is in the Arctic during the Arctic summer and when it turns to winter, migrates to the Antarctic. They are literally flying from one side of the Earth to the other, a journey of at least 12,500 miles. And swallows migrate over thousands of miles every year and go back to the very same place they nested the year before. It's amazing that animals can do this, and no one really knows how.

Best wishes,

Rupert Sheldrake

P.S. I've certainly smelled dog biscuits, but I don't remember ever tasting one . . .

33

Vivien and George walked up Lester's walkway. Lester was waiting on the front steps. Vivien took his hand and pulled him around the back of the house. "Follow us, George," she said.

They crossed the backyard together. Mrs. Robarts was sitting outside in a lawn chair with a cup of tea. The puppy was at her feet, a cute little dog with buff-colored fur.

"Why, he hasn't moved for the past twenty minutes," said Mrs. Robarts. "I would swear he knew you were coming."

George smiled at Lester and Lester smiled back.

Vivien made the introductions. "This is my brother George, Mrs. Robarts," she said. "He loves dogs."

George was already down on the ground petting the puppy. "You're so cute," he said. "What's your name?"

"I call him Sneakers," said Mrs. Robarts. "Because I can't keep up with him despite my shoes." Mrs. Robarts wiggled her feet, which were encased in a pair of red running shoes with white stripes.

George played with Sneakers for a few more minutes while Vivien watched, looking satisfied. Mrs. Robarts made a trip to the toolshed and returned with the bag of dog biscuits. George wondered if she was going to have one with her tea. But she handed the bag to him.

"These are his favorites," she said.

George gave Sneakers a biscuit.

"So what do you think?" asked Vivien.

"I think Sneakers likes me," said George. "And I like him." George had brought a collar and leash just in case. He slipped the collar round Sneakers's neck and attached the leash. "You want to come home with me?" he asked.

Mrs. Robarts clasped her hands in delight. "Isn't this marvelous," she said. "I think Sneakers is going to be very happy. And so will Mr. Robarts."

"Me too," said Vivien, clasping her hands in the same way Mrs. Robarts had.

Sneakers was already tugging George across the lawn. Vivien and Lester followed, Viven taking Lester's hand and giving it a squeeze.

"Thanks, everyone," cried George.

"Oh, thank you," said Mrs. Robarts.

"I guess you can take off your lucky dress now, Viv," said George when they'd gotten home.

"I guess so," sighed Vivien.

Vivien changed into jeans and a sweatshirt. Then she bounced onto George's bed and did a somersault.

"I'm happy," said Vivien.

"Me too," said George.

"See?" said Vivien. "My mantra worked. I think you can catch happiness. Just like you can catch a cold. We caught happiness from Lester and Sneakers. And Mrs. Robarts."

George smiled to himself. Vivien was younger than he was. But sometimes George got the feeling that she knew more about life than he did.

The next day, George took Sneakers to the marsh. He kept the dog on the leash, but that didn't stop Sneakers from dashing madly to and fro chasing birds.

"Hey, little guy," cried George, reeling in the leash. "Take it easy." He'd brought some seeds for Alabaster, but when he got to the outbuilding the pigeon was gone. Instead, Lester was there with Bill Gates. He'd brought a boomerang.

"Hey, I have one of those," said George. "It was a present from Kyra."

"Mine was a present from Bernie," said Lester. "He was my best friend back in Denver."

Sneakers yipped wildly at the sight of Bill Gates. Bill Gates approached the puppy hesitantly, sniffing all the while. Then he sat back patiently and let Sneakers run circles around him.

George and Lester stood on the marsh side by side looking at the empty loft.

"I wonder what made Alabaster leave," said George.

Lester shrugged. "Who knows?" he said. "Maybe that's just how it is. Coming and going. Kind of like a boomerang."

"Maybe," said George.

George sat down on a piece of driftwood. A host of questions had popped into his head. He might never know the answer to them all, but he guessed that was life—how many things there were in the universe that we didn't know and maybe never would.

George looked across the marsh and he felt its flow with all of his senses. Life on the marsh moved ahead— the alewives, the birds. They didn't have regrets, but a faith that at any given moment they were right where they should be.

"I'm really glad you moved here," said George to Lester.

"Me too," said Lester. "Moving is fun." He laughed as he said his mantra. "Change can be positive."

34

Lester and George finished setting up the tent in the Massons' backyard. George pulled back the flaps on either side of the door and secured them. When dusk fell, George's father helped them light a small campfire. George poked hot dogs onto sticks and he and Lester roasted them over the flames.

"Hmmm," said Lester. His mouth had begun to water. "They taste so much better this way."

"They do, don't they?" said George.

When the hot dogs were ready, George squirted his with ketchup and mustard and took a bite. "I think I've become a mustard guy," he said.

"My father said that mustard is an acquired taste," said Lester. He bit into his own hot dog and sat back, breathing in the cool evening air. He could smell the sea wafting in, but it didn't bother him anymore. He now knew that Cape Cod was an acquired taste too.

"Did you ever write to a stranger?" George asked.

"Just Santa Claus," said Lester.

George nodded. "If a stranger wrote you, would you write back?" he said.

"Sure," said Lester.

"Even if you were famous?" said George.

"Yes," said Lester.

George smiled as he thought back to his earlier question—What kind of guy would name his dog Bill Gates? He now knew the answer—The kind of guy who would write to a stranger even if he was famous. The kind of guy that George liked.

Sneakers and Bill Gates had been playing hide-and-seek in the bushes. But when darkness fell they stretched out side by side in front of the tent. George and Lester slipped into their sleeping bags. And George unzipped the window flap in the roof so they could see the stars. There was something mysterious about their twinkling that made George happy. He felt their pull, an unknown force that seemed to tug at him. It reminded him of how vast the universe was, but it made him feel more at home in the world too.

George pointed to the North Star. Then he traced the outline of the Big Dipper. Next to him, Lester was gazing at the same stars.

"Did you know the North Star was how people used to find their way home?" George asked.

"Yes," said Lester. He thought of Denver. "You know

something neat? Everyone in Denver is looking at these same stars."

"And North Carolina," said George, thinking of Kyra and how the stars connected them all. "Weird, isn't it?"

The fortune-teller's words came back to George. He would make an amazing discovery. That didn't seem very prophetic. Amazing discoveries were everywhere just waiting to be found. All you needed was to be curious. Maybe that was the discovery.

Lester sighed. "George, dear," he said, "in life you have to move forward. Maybe that should be my new mantra."

"Yup," said George, agreeing. "In life you have to move forward. Or it could be mine."

Then from an upstairs window in the Massons' house a voice drifted into the night. It was Vivien's and she was chanting her mantra. "Happy all the time," she sang. "Happy all the time."

A Note from Rupert Sheldrake

Dear Reader,

I have enjoyed corresponding with George by e-mail because he's looking at the animals and life-forms around him, thinking about them, and doing something to find out about them. It's not difficult, and it doesn't cost very much, but it's surprising how few people do it. I think it's partly because they assume there's no point because somebody already knows the answers. They probably think that if they are only ten or eleven years old there's nothing they can do to contribute to science or human understanding.

This would be true if we were talking about rocket science or atomic physics or molecular biology. But if we are talking about the mysteries of everyday life, like dogs knowing when their owners are coming home, or feeling when someone is staring at you, or noticing that spiders might respond to your thoughts, it really is possible for someone your age to find out something new. This is partly because scientists haven't explored these areas very much, partly because skeptics have put them off and inhibited the spirit of inquiry.

I hope that George's experience will encourage you to pay attention to animals and to your own experiences, and to think for yourself, and ask questions. Some of them

may be questions like George's, to which no one yet
knows the answers.

With best wishes,

Rupert Sheldrake

BART

DOGS WHO KNOW WHEN THEIR OWNERS ARE COMING HOME
LOGBOOK

PET SPECIES: Dog, part border collie, part mongrel

NAME OF ANIMAL: Bart

AGE AND SEX OF ANIMAL: six in people years; male

NAME OF PERSON MAKING OBSERVATIONS:
George Masson

RELATIONSHIP TO THE PERSON TO WHOM THE ANIMAL
RESPONDS: owner

DATE: Monday, April 15

TIME GEORGE LEFT HOME: 7:25 a.m.

MODE OF TRAVEL: bike

DESTINATION AND DISTANCE: school; 1 mile

TIME GEORGE LEFT SCHOOL: 3:03 p.m.

STOPS ALONG THE WAY: none

TIME GEORGE STARTED FOR HOME: 3:03 p.m.

TIME BART SEEMED TO START WAITING OR ANTICIPATING
GEORGE'S ARRIVAL: 3:05 p.m.

TIME GEORGE ARRIVED HOME: 3:14 p.m.

ANY OTHER COMMENTS OR OBSERVATIONS:

DATE: Tuesday, April 16

TIME GEORGE LEFT HOME: 7:27 a.m.

MODE OF TRAVEL: bike

DESTINATION AND DISTANCE: school; 1 mile

TIME GEORGE LEFT SCHOOL: 3:01 p.m.

STOPS ALONG THE WAY: none

TIME GEORGE STARTED FOR HOME: 3:01 p.m.

TIME BART SEEMED TO START WAITING OR ANTICIPATING GEORGE'S ARRIVAL: 3:02 p.m.

TIME GEORGE ARRIVED HOME: 3:10 p.m.

ANY OTHER COMMENTS OR OBSERVATIONS: I sped home as quickly as I could, arriving a few minutes earlier than I usually would on my bike.

DATE: Wednesday, April 17

TIME GEORGE LEFT HOME: 7:21 a.m.

MODE OF TRAVEL: bike

DESTINATION AND DISTANCE: school; 1 mile

TIME GEORGE LEFT SCHOOL: 3:05 p.m.

STOPS ALONG THE WAY: none

TIME GEORGE STARTED FOR HOME: 3:05 p.m.

TIME BART SEEMED TO START WAITING OR ANTICIPATING GEORGE'S ARRIVAL: 3:10 p.m.

TIME GEORGE ARRIVED HOME: 3:22 p.m.

ANY OTHER COMMENTS OR OBSERVATIONS:

DATE: Thursday, April 18

TIME GEORGE LEFT HOME: 7:24 a.m.

MODE OF TRAVEL: foot

DESTINATION AND DISTANCE: school; 1 mile

TIME GEORGE LEFT SCHOOL: 3:16 p.m.

STOPS ALONG THE WAY: dentist

TIME GEORGE STARTED FOR HOME (FROM THE DENTIST):
4:01 p.m.

TIME BART SEEMED TO START WAITING OR ANTICIPATING
GEORGE'S ARRIVAL: 4:04 p.m.

TIME GEORGE ARRIVED HOME: 4:12 p.m.

ANY OTHER COMMENTS OR OBSERVATIONS: Bart seemed
to know that I wasn't coming right home after school. But he seemed
to pick up on my intention to come home after my dentist
appointment.

DATE: Friday, April 19

TIME GEORGE LEFT HOME: 7:24 a.m.

MODE OF TRAVEL: bike

DESTINATION AND DISTANCE: school; 1 mile

TIME GEORGE LEFT SCHOOL: 3:03 p.m.

STOPS ALONG THE WAY: none

TIME GEORGE STARTED FOR HOME: 3:03 p.m.

TIME BART SEEMED TO START WAITING OR ANTICIPATING GEORGE'S ARRIVAL: 3:09 p.m.

TIME GEORGE ARRIVED HOME: 3:15 p.m.

ANY OTHER COMMENTS OR OBSERVATIONS:

DATE: Monday, April 22

TIME GEORGE LEFT HOME: 7:30 a.m.

MODE OF TRAVEL: bike

DESTINATION AND DISTANCE: school; 1 mile

TIME GEORGE LEFT SCHOOL: 3:05 p.m.

STOPS ALONG THE WAY: planned stop at the bike shop

TIME GEORGE STARTED FOR HOME (FROM THE BIKE SHOP): 3:30 p.m.

TIME BART SEEMED TO START WAITING OR ANTICIPATING GEORGE'S ARRIVAL: 3:35 p.m.

TIME GEORGE ARRIVED HOME: 3:43 p.m.

ANY OTHER COMMENTS OR OBSERVATIONS: I made a planned stop at the bike shop and Bart started waiting not when I left school but 5 minutes after I left the bike shop. But 3 minutes before I arrived, he was distracted by a mole and ran off after it.

DATE: Tuesday, April 23

TIME GEORGE LEFT HOME: 7:28 a.m.

MODE OF TRAVEL: bike

DESTINATION AND DISTANCE: school; 1 mile

TIME GEORGE LEFT SCHOOL: 3:04 p.m.

STOPS ALONG THE WAY: none

TIME GEORGE STARTED FOR HOME: 3:04 p.m.

TIME BART SEEMED TO START WAITING OR ANTICIPATING
GEORGE'S ARRIVAL: 3:08 p.m.

TIME GEORGE ARRIVED HOME: 3:16 p.m.

ANY OTHER COMMENTS OR OBSERVATIONS:

DATE: Wednesday, April 24

TIME GEORGE LEFT HOME: 7:30 a.m.

MODE OF TRAVEL: foot

DESTINATION AND DISTANCE: school; 1 mile

TIME GEORGE LEFT SCHOOL: 3:02 p.m.

STOPS ALONG THE WAY: none

TIME GEORGE STARTED FOR HOME: 3:02 p.m.

TIME BART SEEMED TO START WAITING OR ANTICIPATING
GEORGE'S ARRIVAL: 3:07 p.m.

TIME GEORGE ARRIVED HOME: 3:27 p.m.

ANY OTHER COMMENTS OR OBSERVATIONS:

DATE: Thursday, April 25

TIME GEORGE LEFT HOME: 7:20 a.m.

MODE OF TRAVEL: foot

DESTINATION AND DISTANCE: school; 1 mile

TIME GEORGE LEFT SCHOOL: 3:04 p.m.

STOPS ALONG THE WAY: none

TIME GEORGE STARTED FOR HOME: 3:04 p.m.

TIME BART SEEMED TO START WAITING OR ANTICIPATING
GEORGE'S ARRIVAL: 3:09 p.m.

TIME GEORGE ARRIVED HOME: 3:38 p.m.

ANY OTHER COMMENTS OR OBSERVATIONS: I set the intent
to leave school for home, but I slowed down my pace so that it
took me significantly longer than usual.

DATE: Friday, April 26

TIME GEORGE LEFT HOME: 7:32 a.m.

MODE OF TRAVEL: bike

DESTINATION AND DISTANCE: school; 1 mile

TIME GEORGE LEFT SCHOOL: 3:02 p.m.

STOPS ALONG THE WAY: none

TIME GEORGE STARTED FOR HOME: 3:02 p.m.

TIME BART SEEMED TO START WAITING OR ANTICIPATING
GEORGE'S ARRIVAL: 3:05 p.m.

TIME GEORGE ARRIVED HOME: 3:14 p.m.

ANY OTHER COMMENTS OR OBSERVATIONS:

DATE: Monday, April 29

TIME GEORGE LEFT HOME: 7:29 a.m.

MODE OF TRAVEL: foot

DESTINATION AND DISTANCE: school; 1 mile

TIME GEORGE LEFT SCHOOL: 3:15 p.m.

STOPS ALONG THE WAY: drop Vivien at dance class, chat with
Lester

TIME GEORGE STARTED FOR HOME (FROM DANCING SCHOOL): 3:30 p.m.

TIME BART SEEMED TO START WAITING OR ANTICIPATING GEORGE'S ARRIVAL: 3:30 p.m.

TIME GEORGE ARRIVED HOME: 3:45 p.m.

ANY OTHER COMMENTS OR OBSERVATIONS: I got home much later than I normally would, but Bart came to wait when I left Vivien's dancing school and started home.

DATE: Tuesday, April 30

TIME GEORGE LEFT HOME: 7:26 a.m.

MODE OF TRAVEL: bike

DESTINATION AND DISTANCE: school; 1 mile

TIME GEORGE LEFT SCHOOL: 3:08 p.m.

STOPS ALONG THE WAY: stopped at Lester's house

TIME GEORGE STARTED FOR HOME (FROM LESTER'S HOUSE): 5:25 p.m.

TIME BART SEEMED TO START WAITING OR ANTICIPATING GEORGE'S ARRIVAL: 5:24 p.m.

TIME GEORGE ARRIVED HOME: 5:30 p.m.

ANY OTHER COMMENTS OR OBSERVATIONS: Bart didn't come out to the steps until well after 5 p.m., so he seemed to know that I wasn't coming directly home from school.

DATE: Wednesday, May 1

TIME GEORGE LEFT HOME: 7:31 a.m.

MODE OF TRAVEL: bike

DESTINATION AND DISTANCE: school; 1 mile

TIME GEORGE LEFT SCHOOL: 3:03 p.m.

STOPS ALONG THE WAY: none

TIME GEORGE STARTED FOR HOME: 3:03 p.m.

TIME BART SEEMED TO START WAITING OR ANTICIPATING GEORGE'S ARRIVAL: 3:07 p.m.

TIME GEORGE ARRIVED HOME: 3:20 p.m.

ANY OTHER COMMENTS OR OBSERVATIONS:

DATE: Thursday, May 2

TIME GEORGE LEFT HOME: 7:24 a.m.

MODE OF TRAVEL: bike

DESTINATION AND DISTANCE: school; 1 mile

TIME GEORGE LEFT SCHOOL: 2:45 p.m.

STOPS ALONG THE WAY: none

TIME GEORGE STARTED FOR HOME: 2:45 p.m.

TIME BART SEEMED TO START WAITING OR ANTICIPATING
GEORGE'S ARRIVAL: 2:49 p.m.

TIME GEORGE ARRIVED HOME: 2:56 p.m.

ANY OTHER COMMENTS OR OBSERVATIONS:

DATE: Friday, May 3

TIME GEORGE LEFT HOME: 7:30 a.m.

MODE OF TRAVEL: foot

DESTINATION AND DISTANCE: school; 1 mile

TIME GEORGE LEFT SCHOOL: 3:03 p.m.

STOPS ALONG THE WAY: went to look for Vivien

TIME GEORGE STARTED FOR HOME: 3:30 p.m. after I found
Vivien

TIME BART SEEMED TO START WAITING OR ANTICIPATING
GEORGE'S ARRIVAL: Bart wasn't waiting

TIME GEORGE ARRIVED HOME: 3:40 p.m.

ANY OTHER COMMENTS OR OBSERVATIONS: Bart wasn't

waiting, and I think it could be that my intention to start home was interrupted when I couldn't find Vivien. I had to look for her and couldn't think of going home.

BILL GATES

DOGS WHO KNOW WHEN THEIR OWNERS ARE COMING HOME

LOGBOOK

PET SPECIES: Dog, part golden retriever, part mongrel

NAME OF ANIMAL: Bill Gates

AGE AND SEX OF ANIMAL: seven in people years; male

NAME OF PERSON MAKING OBSERVATIONS:
Lester Shoe

RELATIONSHIP TO THE PERSON TO WHOM THE ANIMAL
RESPONDS: owner

DATE: Tuesday, April 16

TIME LESTER LEFT HOME: 7:32 a.m.

MODE OF TRAVEL: bike

DESTINATION AND DISTANCE: school; ¾ mile

TIME LESTER LEFT SCHOOL: 3:01 p.m.

STOPS ALONG THE WAY: none

TIME LESTER STARTED FOR HOME: 3:01 p.m.

TIME BILL GATES SEEMED TO START WAITING OR
ANTICIPATING LESTER'S ARRIVAL: Bill Gates wasn't waiting

TIME LESTER ARRIVED HOME: 3:11 p.m.

ANY OTHER COMMENTS OR OBSERVATIONS: I realized I wasn't
very focused when thinking of home.

DATE: Wednesday, April 17

TIME LESTER LEFT HOME: 7:20 a.m.

MODE OF TRAVEL: foot

DESTINATION AND DISTANCE: school; ¾ mile

TIME LESTER LEFT SCHOOL: 3:03 p.m.

STOPS ALONG THE WAY: none

TIME LESTER STARTED FOR HOME: 3:03 p.m.

TIME BILL GATES SEEMED TO START WAITING OR ANTICIPATING LESTER'S ARRIVAL: 3:05 p.m.

TIME LESTER ARRIVED HOME: 3:24 p.m.

ANY OTHER COMMENTS OR OBSERVATIONS: I was very precise in my intention to set out for my new home on Cape Cod.

DATE: Thursday, April 18

TIME LESTER LEFT HOME: 7:35 a.m.

MODE OF TRAVEL: bike

DESTINATION AND DISTANCE: school; ¾ mile

TIME LESTER LEFT SCHOOL: 3:16 p.m.

STOPS ALONG THE WAY: none

TIME LESTER STARTED FOR HOME: 3:16 p.m.

TIME BILL GATES SEEMED TO START WAITING OR ANTICIPATING LESTER'S ARRIVAL: 3:20 p.m.

TIME LESTER ARRIVED HOME: 3:27 p.m.

ANY OTHER COMMENTS OR OBSERVATIONS: I hung around school for about 15 minutes before starting home and Bill Gates seemed to be responding to this because he went out to the gate later than he might have if I'd gone straight home.

DATE: Friday, April 19

TIME LESTER LEFT HOME: 7:32 a.m.

MODE OF TRAVEL: foot

DESTINATION AND DISTANCE: school; ¾ mile

TIME LESTER LEFT SCHOOL: 3:20 p.m.

STOPS ALONG THE WAY: unplanned stop in front of neighbor's

TIME LESTER STARTED FOR HOME: 3:20 p.m.

TIME BILL GATES SEEMED TO START WAITING OR
ANTICIPATING LESTER'S ARRIVAL: 3:41 p.m.

TIME LESTER ARRIVED HOME: 3:45 p.m.

ANY OTHER COMMENTS OR OBSERVATIONS: I purposefully
increased the time it took me to walk home. I hung around the
playground awhile and then made a stop in front of the
neighbor's house. But Bill Gates was not fooled. He came out to
the gate right after I set the intention to head home.

DATE: Monday, April 22

TIME LESTER LEFT HOME: 7:33 a.m.

MODE OF TRAVEL: foot

DESTINATION AND DISTANCE: school; ¾ mile

TIME LESTER LEFT SCHOOL: 3:10 p.m.

STOPS ALONG THE WAY: none

TIME LESTER STARTED FOR HOME: 3:10 p.m.

TIME BILL GATES SEEMED TO START WAITING OR
ANTICIPATING LESTER'S ARRIVAL: 3:13 p.m.

TIME LESTER ARRIVED HOME: 3:42 p.m.

ANY OTHER COMMENTS OR OBSERVATIONS: I took a longer
route home, but Bill Gates still went out to wait within minutes of
when I left school.

DATE: Tuesday, April 23

TIME LESTER LEFT HOME: 7:35 a.m.

MODE OF TRAVEL: bike

DESTINATION AND DISTANCE: school; 3/4 mile

TIME LESTER LEFT SCHOOL: 3:00 p.m.

STOPS ALONG THE WAY: none

TIME LESTER STARTED FOR HOME: 3:00 p.m.

TIME BILL GATES SEEMED TO START WAITING OR
ANTICIPATING LESTER'S ARRIVAL: 3:00 p.m.

TIME LESTER ARRIVED HOME: 3:09 p.m.

ANY OTHER COMMENTS OR OBSERVATIONS:

DATE: Wednesday, April 24

TIME LESTER LEFT HOME: 7:32 a.m.

MODE OF TRAVEL: foot

DESTINATION AND DISTANCE: school; ¾ mile

TIME LESTER LEFT SCHOOL: 3:04 p.m.

STOPS ALONG THE WAY: stopped at the playground

TIME LESTER STARTED FOR HOME (FROM PLAYGROUND):
3:43 p.m.

TIME BILL GATES SEEMED TO START WAITING OR
ANTICIPATING LESTER'S ARRIVAL: 3:48 p.m.

TIME LESTER ARRIVED HOME: 3:55 p.m.

ANY OTHER COMMENTS OR OBSERVATIONS: I doubled the time
it would normally take me to walk home, but Bill Gates seemed to
respond to when I started home from the park.

DATE: Thursday, April 25

TIME LESTER LEFT HOME: 7:28 a.m.

MODE OF TRAVEL: foot

DESTINATION AND DISTANCE: school; ¾ mile

TIME LESTER LEFT SCHOOL: 3:02 p.m.

STOPS ALONG THE WAY: bus station

TIME LESTER STARTED FOR HOME (FROM THE BUS STATION):
3:28 p.m.

TIME BILL GATES SEEMED TO START WAITING OR
ANTICIPATING LESTER'S ARRIVAL: 3:31 p.m.

TIME LESTER ARRIVED HOME: 3:45 p.m.

ANY OTHER COMMENTS OR OBSERVATIONS: I arrived home
later than normal because I stopped at the bus station. Bill
Gates seemed to be responding to the time I left the station.

DATE: Friday, April 26

TIME LESTER LEFT HOME: 7:25 a.m.

MODE OF TRAVEL: bike

DESTINATION AND DISTANCE: school; ¾ mile

TIME LESTER LEFT SCHOOL: 3:02 p.m.

STOPS ALONG THE WAY: none

TIME LESTER STARTED FOR HOME: 3:02 p.m.

TIME BILL GATES SEEMED TO START WAITING OR
ANTICIPATING LESTER'S ARRIVAL: 3:06 p.m.

TIME LESTER ARRIVED HOME: 3:16 p.m.

ANY OTHER COMMENTS OR OBSERVATIONS:

DATE: Monday, April 29

TIME LESTER LEFT HOME: 7:30 a.m.

MODE OF TRAVEL: foot

DESTINATION AND DISTANCE: school; ¾ mile

TIME LESTER LEFT SCHOOL: 3:15 p.m.

STOPS ALONG THE WAY: none

TIME LESTER STARTED FOR HOME: 3:15 p.m.

TIME BILL GATES SEEMED TO START WAITING OR
ANTICIPATING LESTER'S ARRIVAL: 3:20 p.m.

TIME LESTER ARRIVED HOME: 3:45 p.m.

ANY OTHER COMMENTS OR OBSERVATIONS: I started home
from school nearly 15 minutes later than I normally would, and
walked slowly. And Bill Gates came out to the gate nearly
15 minutes later than he normally would.

DATE: Tuesday, April 30

TIME LESTER LEFT HOME: 7:24 a.m.

MODE OF TRAVEL: bike

DESTINATION AND DISTANCE: school; ¾ mile

TIME LESTER LEFT SCHOOL: 3:08 p.m.

STOPS ALONG THE WAY: none

TIME LESTER STARTED FOR HOME: 3:08 p.m.

TIME BILL GATES SEEMED TO START WAITING OR
ANTICIPATING LESTER'S ARRIVAL: 3:07 p.m.

TIME LESTER ARRIVED HOME: 3:34 p.m.

ANY OTHER COMMENTS OR OBSERVATIONS: George came over
to my house after school. But that didn't change Bill Gates's
behavior. He seemed to know when I was coming, and came out
just before I left school. I may have already been thinking about
getting home before leaving school as George was coming
with me.

DATE: Wednesday, May 1

TIME LESTER LEFT HOME: 7:26 a.m.

MODE OF TRAVEL: bike

DESTINATION AND DISTANCE: school; ¾ mile

TIME LESTER LEFT SCHOOL: 3:03 p.m.

STOPS ALONG THE WAY: none

TIME LESTER STARTED FOR HOME: 3:03 p.m.

TIME BILL GATES SEEMED TO START WAITING OR
ANTICIPATING LESTER'S ARRIVAL: 3:06 p.m.

TIME LESTER ARRIVED HOME: 3:21 p.m.

ANY OTHER COMMENTS OR OBSERVATIONS:

DATE: Thursday, May 2

TIME LESTER LEFT HOME: 7:33 a.m.

MODE OF TRAVEL: bike

DESTINATION AND DISTANCE: school; ¾ mile

TIME LESTER LEFT SCHOOL: 2:45 p.m.

STOPS ALONG THE WAY: none

TIME LESTER STARTED FOR HOME: 2:45 p.m.

TIME BILL GATES SEEMED TO START WAITING OR
ANTICIPATING LESTER'S ARRIVAL: 2:50 p.m.

TIME LESTER ARRIVED HOME: 2:55 p.m.

ANY OTHER COMMENTS OR OBSERVATIONS:

DATE: Friday, May 3

TIME LESTER LEFT HOME: 7:30 a.m.

MODE OF TRAVEL: foot

DESTINATION AND DISTANCE: school; ¾ mile

TIME LESTER LEFT SCHOOL: 3:05 p.m.

STOPS ALONG THE WAY: none

TIME LESTER STARTED FOR HOME: 3:05 p.m.

TIME BILL GATES SEEMED TO START WAITING OR
ANTICIPATING LESTER'S ARRIVAL: 3:07 p.m.

TIME LESTER ARRIVED HOME: 3:27 p.m.

ANY OTHER COMMENTS OR OBSERVATIONS:

DATE: Monday, May 6

TIME LESTER LEFT HOME: 7:35 a.m.

MODE OF TRAVEL: foot

DESTINATION AND DISTANCE: school; ¾ mile

TIME LESTER LEFT SCHOOL: 3:03 p.m.

STOPS ALONG THE WAY: I took a detour past George's house

TIME LESTER STARTED FOR HOME: 3:33 p.m.

TIME BILL GATES SEEMED TO START WAITING OR
ANTICIPATING LESTER'S ARRIVAL: He wasn't waiting

TIME LESTER ARRIVED HOME: 3:40 p.m.

ANY OTHER COMMENTS OR OBSERVATIONS:

DATE: Tuesday, May 7

TIME LESTER LEFT HOME: 7:32 a.m.

MODE OF TRAVEL: foot

DESTINATION AND DISTANCE: school; ¾ mile

TIME LESTER LEFT SCHOOL: 3:06 p.m.

STOPS ALONG THE WAY: none

TIME LESTER STARTED FOR HOME: 3:06 p.m.

TIME BILL GATES SEEMED TO START WAITING OR
ANTICIPATING LESTER'S ARRIVAL: Bill Gates wasn't there

TIME LESTER ARRIVED HOME: 3:41 p.m.

ANY OTHER COMMENTS OR OBSERVATIONS: Bill Gates came
out to the walkway several times during the day—the last time at
2:51 p.m. But he wasn't there when I got home. I didn't feel well
because I had just found out about George's dog. So maybe Bill
Gates was responding to that.